Copyright © 2024 by Meg Smitherman

All rights reserved.

No part of this book may be reproduced in any form or by any electronic or mechanical means, including information storage and retrieval systems, without written permission from the author, except for the use of brief quotations in a book review.

Editor: Page & Proof

Covert art: Nastya Litepla

Cover design: Adam Wayne

❦ Created with Vellum

ALSO BY MEG SMITHERMAN

Destroyer

Sanctifier

The Frost Queen's Blade

CONTENT NOTE

- Body horror
- Psychological horror
- Sex scenes where the protagonist is confused/afraid/psychologically impaired (but still otherwise consenting)
- Implied toxic/abusive family dynamics (off-page, takes place in the past)

THRUM

MEG SMITHERMAN

ROSE & MOTH BOOKS

I have desired to go
Where springs not fail,
To fields where flies no sharp and sided hail,
And a few lilies blow.

And I have asked to be
Where no storms come,
Where the green swell is in the havens dumb,
And out of the swing of the sea.

Gerard Manley-Hopkins
Heaven-Haven (a nun takes the veil)

1

MY FIRST THOUGHT is that my crew is sleeping. All three of them, peaceful, eyes closed against the still air. And if I leave them here, eventually they'll come traipsing one by one into the galley for cups of bitter dehydrated coffee, happily bitching and jostling in that cramped space. But their chests don't rise and fall. Their eyes don't move under the lids to indicate a dream cycle. And their faces, as much as I try to rationalize it — their faces are gray and mask-like, nearly unrecognizable.

The crew of the *Pioneer* has been dead for a long time. I'm the only one left. We made it to our destination, and I'm the only one left.

This realization doesn't hit me like a blow; it seeps into me, slow. Like the inevitable pull of a deep current, my body tossed by swift waters. When the brain begins to gasp for oxygen. When the senses dull and inevitability takes hold. Like shutting down.

All around me the white walls close in. The sharp smell of antiseptic and recycled air threatens to choke me.

I'd rather I could smell *them*. I'd rather their rotten flesh gag me in its decomposition than feel separate from them, as if they might still be alive somehow, trapped in stasis for eternity.

I remember what we learned in training: the chance of death during stasis was small enough, they'd said, that it was worth the risk. This mission was worth the risk.

Their calculations must have been wrong.

It happens. This is deep space and not the first manned mission beyond Earth. But it is the first to move beyond Sol, to seek the reaches of the cosmos beyond our star. It takes years to get out of the Sol system, and even longer to get to the next system over, which is where we are. Where I am. Space, of course, is bigger than anyone comprehends, bigger than the human mind can handle. We're able to come to some understanding of it with mathematics, and philosophy, and even art. We can look at pictures, read comparisons, and conduct complex equations to try to make sense of it.

But the fact is that the biological makeup of a human brain is too simple, its neurons too few, to understand the true enormity of our universe. It is incalculably and emphatically beyond us.

Thank God for that.

I look down at Lily for a long time, the papery skin at the edges of her eyes. Her red-brown hair is still glossy; I remember she'd washed it before we departed. She'd said she wanted to look nice after sleeping for several years. As our psych officer, she was supposed to help with situations like this. If something went wrong, if we started to feel the strange psychological effects of deep space travel (and we would), it would have been her job to talk to us about it. Work through it. Medicate us, if it came to that.

I can't stop thinking about the way she used to wind her hair into a messy bun, how pieces used to always fall free around her face.

I'll have to find my own drugs, now.

I don't remember coming out of stasis, the excruciating process of it. That's both by design and a quirk of the human brain, we had been told. Being essentially frozen in a dreamless state for years isn't normal. Lily had said the amnesia wears off eventually, and by then, you're recovered enough to handle it: The memory of waking. She'd described it as a sort of second birth. A horrible, painful wrenching from a drift in nothingness, from a peaceful emptiness into the screaming-bright now. We are infants after stasis: helpless, naked, and wailing.

I'm glad I don't remember it. I hope I never do.

Mahdi lies next to Lily. I study him, too, his peaceful expression. His full black beard is exactly the length it was when we left Earth, his skin as smooth and brown. As if he never aged, never died. Stasis freezes you like that.

My mind — against my will — goes to my brother. I wonder if Henry ever grew the mustache he wanted to, or if his upper lip remained bare but for the few scattered hairs he had carefully maintained for most of his adult life, in the vain hope of more.

I remember some of his last words to me, his sad smile. "I hope you find what you're looking for, MiMi."

But Henry would be an old man now, thanks to special relativistic time dilation. And by the time I return to Earth, if I'm granted that grace, my brother will be long dead.

There's nothing I can do with the emotion that overtakes me in a swell, threatening to undo me. So I take a deep breath and pack it away, setting it aside for later. I can't right now. I don't have the strength.

Finally, I move to the last stasis pod and say a silent farewell to Vasilissa. She and I never got along. She was argumentative, self-righteous, and always said my introversion was going to be a liability on the mission. Well, assholes are liabilities too. But in death, she has faded to a shadow of herself, and a pang catches in my chest. I'd do anything to be at the receiving end of one more of her dagger-sharp glares.

A repetitive sound pings in my ears, high-pitched and unrelenting. I realize it's been going off for some time now. I tear my impotent gaze from the bodies, still zipped up snug in their stasis pods, and go thoughtlessly toward the sound.

I think I'm in shock.

I climb up a ladder on my way to the cockpit, where I'm sure the alarm is sounding. I pass through the galley on my way. It's dark, empty. Of course it is. Did I expect to see someone there, heating up water? Did I expect to hear laughter, to see my crew? It is a dead space, a circular coffin of a room in a coffin of a ship.

A heavy stone settles in my stomach.

I continue up the ladder, focusing on the now. On what needs to be done. It occurs to me that I'm strangely spry for someone who just woke up from stasis. The sleep should have taken a toll on my agility, if not my muscle mass. Electrodes kept our muscles from atrophying, but it should have taken days for me to regain my strength.

Yet here I am, flying up a ladder as if it's nothing. Spurred by grief, perhaps. Or maybe the scientists got it wrong. They got the survival rate wrong, somehow. I don't want to think about what else they might have fucked up.

The cockpit is small, just big enough for two if we didn't mind being crammed together. A sharp pain twinges in my chest. A cramped cockpit is a problem for another universe, one where Lily and Mahdi and Vasilissa are alive. I settle myself in one of the tiny swiveling chairs and scan the dash. For a moment, I'm overwhelmed with sensory input — buttons, lights, screens, readouts. My head spins, and I bend over, swallowing bile.

The alarm sound continues.

"You're fine, Ami," I say, almost scolding, as if I'm a wayward child. "You know this."

I take a few deep breaths, the way Lily taught us — four seconds in, hold it for three, and eight seconds out. Something about the vagus nerve, lowering anxiety, that kind of thing. I take a second to wish, fervently, that she was here with me. That she was leaning over me, arms wrapped around my shoulders, her voice in my ear, her hair tickling my cheek. A lump forms in my throat.

"You're fine," I say again. It's less convincing this time.

At last, the dash controls resolve into something I understand. I know these symbols, these buttons and readouts. I *learned* it in training. But I'm not supposed to be in this situation; Mahdi was both pilot and engineer. The rest of us were only trained in case he... He should have been the one...

The thought stutters, and I close my eyes. I'm here now. I can't look back.

The alarm screams and screams.

I swallow hard. Stop the alarm, that's all. One thing at a time, and the first thing is to stop the alarm.

Scanning the controls, I see it: a throbbing red pulse on the diagnostic screen. It's a malfunction. No, *two* malfunctions, both triggering the alarm. One is located at the fuel tank, the other at our comms array.

"*Pioneer*," I say.

`Yes, Ms. Selwyn.`

I'm taken by the ridiculous urge to ask the ship computer to address me by my given name. Ms. Selwyn sounds old, like someone on her way to death. "Diagnostic summary, please."

`Fuel reserves are at a critical low. The long-range communications array is nonfunctional.`

I wait, but *Pioneer* seems finished with the diagnostic. "I need more information than that, *Pioneer*. Why are the fuel reserves low? We should only have used a fraction of it." As I ask the question, I check our trajectory and see we're exactly where we'd planned to be. Well, close enough. We've drifted a bit further than we should have, just beyond the outermost planet in this system, but that's all.

`I have located an external leak. A hull breach.` She reads out some coordinates, an exact location on the hull, but I'm barely comprehending. I nod as if I understand. As if this has sunk in.

"What caused it?"

`Unknown.`

"And the comms array? What happened there?"

`An unknown hardware malfunction.`

"So it's... broken."

No answer. Wonderful. Our comms array is out of commission, and there's a breach in the hull. There's not supposed to be significant debris in this pocket of space, but we did veer off course. And deep space probes are known to be fallible. Maybe a meteoroid, or some chunk of space rock, hurtled through our comms and the hull like a bullet.

"*Pioneer*," I say, "can you tell me when these malfunctions occurred?"

`The hull breach occurred at 0439 hours this morning. The communications array malfunctioned at 0502 hours this morning.`

So recently. And twenty-three minutes apart.

Two meteoroids, then.

I stare at the diagnostic screen as if looking at it will lead to comprehension. As if by looking at those two pulsing dots hard enough, I might bring my crew back to life, fix the ship, and set everything to rights. My mouth tastes sharply of bile, and I swallow roughly.

The alarm sounds.

"Turn that thing off, *Pioneer*," I snap.

`Disabling the alarm.`

In the following silence, my ears ring as if the alarm is still shrieking, unending, unstoppable, echoing forever in the darkness of my mind.

I consider going outside to attempt to fix the hull breach and quickly realize the futility of it. I'm not going anywhere fast. *Pioneer* is practically at a dead stop, relying on inertia to keep her going unless I fire up the engines. But that won't happen without any fuel. My priority is the comms array. If there's anyone out here at the edge of the system, God willing, a distress signal might save me.

In training, they went over the probability of us finding intelligent life in Sol's neighboring systems. It was as close to zero as a number can get without being utterly zilch, but it was still a high enough number that a few Earth governments joined forces to make this mission happen. That tiny number used to fill me with this vibrating eagerness, an aching hope, the need to see and understand and *know* what lay so far beyond us.

Now, that number is the reason I'm going to die out here. Alone.

2

JUST BEFORE I suit up to fix the comms array, I completely lose my shit.

It comes all at once: the panic, the horror, the grief, the knowledge that I am utterly, utterly alone. The dam breaks and floods me so I can't hear or see or think; I'm awash with pain, and there's nothing to hold on to as it drowns me.

I slide to the floor just outside the airlock, curl myself around my knees, and try not to pass out. My breathing is too fast, too shallow. I know this, distantly. But no matter how many times I try Lily's breathing technique, I can't stop gasping. I'm running out of air, or gulping too much of it, I can't tell. Tears stream down my face, but I don't remember allowing myself to cry. My chest lurches in painful hiccups. My vision blurs.

I'm hyperventilating. The thought comes from far away: *this is a panic attack. Alert.* But the thought is so far away that it's unreachable.

Lily would have clicked her tongue at me. "Remember

what I taught you," she'd say. "We, as humans, too often forget what grounds us to the physical world, to our own bodies. When you think about breathing, you forge a connection with yourself. When you control that breathing, the connection grows stronger. And you begin to find peace."

I just — I can't stop thinking about them, how we all got into those pods together, eyes shining with anticipation. Knowing we'd wake up together, too. We were going to make history, we said. The four of us were going to discover life in other systems. We were going to change the world.

I can't even connect with myself. How am I supposed to connect with an alien lifeform? The mission is over. I can't do it on my own. I can't. I can't.

My vision darkens at the edges. I need to slow my breathing, or I'll lose consciousness. Finally, I bury my wet face in the crook of my elbow, hoping to cut off my access to oxygen. The paper bag method, but for girls adrift in deep space. When the vivid black and yellow spots in my vision finally begin to fade, I sit up, drenched in tears and snot.

I draw a slow breath, the way Lily taught us. Then I struggle to my feet.

"You're fine, Ami."

I stand before the spacesuit, gazing into its reflective helmet. Something in me wants to speak to it, wants to comfort myself with this human-shaped carapace, this thing that will keep me warm and breathing and alive when I open the door to the universe.

But it's only a spacesuit. And all I see is my own face staring back at me, blotchy and tear-stained, with strands of jet-black hair clinging to my sweaty skin. I'm sickly pale, but for the angry red that mars my cheeks, and the bloodshot whites of my eyes. I find no comfort in my reflection. She's a stranger to me.

Slowly, meticulously, with a touch of paranoia, I begin to pull on the spacesuit. I check it more than a dozen times — every joint, every fastening. I check the oxygen tank over and over, obsessively. I check my biometrics, again and again. We're meant to do this in teams. One person helps their partner suit up, and vice versa.

But I'm alone.

So I check, and check again, until I'm certain the suit won't fly apart the second I'm in zero pressure, condemning me to a swift and horrific death in the vacuum of space. But my heart doesn't slow. It's a relentless thing, loud in my chest, uncontrollable, and far too fast.

"You're f-fine."

I've done this a million times in training. Under water, in simulations, all of it. So many times I couldn't begin to count. I know what I'm doing.

But that doesn't make it easier, stepping into space. All alone, with only a tether to hold me in place, only molecules and fibers and inorganic material to trust.

I wish someone, anyone, even Vasilissa — I wish she was here. She was fearless. An asshole, but fearless.

"*Pioneer*," I say, "I'm going out. To fix the comms array." I'm not sure what to say next. What does the ship care if I'm gone? If I never come back? "You may need to talk me through it," I finally add.

`Affirmative.`

I clamber into the airlock. The suit isn't incredibly bulky, but I'm not used to it in the artificial grav. It weighs me down. My chest tightens, dread rising in my throat.

No, no. I'm okay. It'll only take a few minutes.

The act of closing the airlock door behind me, sealing myself inside what will soon become a vacuum, feels interminable. As if I'm in slow motion, the heavy bulkhead door is like the portcullis of an ancient stronghold, and I'm about to turn myself over to the invading army.

When the door is safely sealed, I go to the control panel. It's not complex; everything on this ship is as simple and hard-wired as the engineers could manage, lessening the possibility of tech failure. I study the panel's square buttons and an antiquated display showing the airlock's air pressure status. It's equal with the interior of the rest of the ship.

I press one of the square buttons with an awkwardly suited finger, and the airlock begins to lose pressure. I drift slowly up as the air leaves this liminal space, this breath before I give myself up to the vastness of space and God, and then there's a decisive *beep!* from the panel.

It's safe to open the outer door. I tether myself to the ship using heavy-duty clamps, giving myself just enough slack in the tether, everything exactly as we learned. If I just do these things by rote, surely I can't make a mistake. Nothing else will go wrong. After testing my lifeline, I wish I'd had a drink of water; my mouth tastes like bile.

And I don't want to go outside. But I'm all that's left. I have to do it, or accept that I'll die out here.

So I step into the black.

I'm drifting half out of the ship, half in, but even then it feels as if the infinite universe is reaching for me with inexorable fingers, with hands made of whorls of starlight, of depthless lightless chasms that hum like monsters of the cosmos. The air in my lungs feels like a dare. I'm challenging the firmament in its horrible power, and it is gazing right back at me, unimpressed.

I grab the line, wrapping my suited hand through the tether. I swivel my head as much as I can and see, with a sickening swoop of the gut, that I've drifted a few yards from the ship. I'm surrounded by nothingness; if I were to cut the tether, I would drift out here until I ran out of oxygen, suffocating in my suit.

Heart in my throat, I pull myself back to the ship, clutching at one of the outer handholds. I breathe deeply. "Don't hyperventilate," I say, unable to ignore the quaver in my voice. "You need the oxygen."

Somehow, I manage to breathe evenly and pull myself hand over hand along the hull of the ship. As I approach the comms array, its delicate silhouette of metal shining brightly in the starlight, I see how damaged it really is. It looks as if a piece of it is missing. Not bent out of shape or damaged, but missing, like a branch snapped from a tree.

I suppose a meteoroid could have done this. A lot of things could have done this.

I finally reach the array and fasten myself to it using heavy-duty hooks and the slack in my tether. "*Pioneer*," I say. "Are you seeing this?"

`Affirmative. The camera on your helmet is operational.`

"I meant the broken array, smartass," I reply, indulging in rudeness, petulance. Sweat beads on my upper lip.

`Affirmative. It has been damaged.`

I glower at the array, trying to make sense of it. I peer at the place where there should be evidence of a break. Of metal snapping away from metal. Instead, I see serrated lines, regularly spaced. "How was it damaged?" I demand.

`It appears to have been snapped off by space debris.`

I squint. "No, look at the ridges. Someone, something — it's been sawed off." The words are so small on my tongue, just syllables, but I feel like I've swallowed poison and spat it out, coating my mouth with slow death.

Pioneer says nothing.

"*Pioneer*," I insist. "Look. Do you see that? It wasn't snapped off. The metal would be smooth. It's been cut."

`Negative`, says *Pioneer*. The comms array was snapped off by space debris.

"*Look!*" I say again, tapping the metal. "That's not a snap."

Pioneer says nothing.

I wait for a moment, breath heavy in my lungs, throat tight. There's no use arguing with a ship. The camera on my helmet must be positively antiquated. "Fine," I relent. "How do I fix this, then?"

`It cannot be fixed without the missing part.`

A chill grips me. "Surely I can improvise."

`Negative.`

"Tell me what I *can* do," I say, voice shaking. I'm almost halfway through my suit's oxygen reserve.

There's a long moment of silence. At last, *Pioneer* says, `I have calculated for every possible mode` of repair with the aim to communicate long-distance. There are none. The missing part is necessary for long-distance communications.

I can feel sweat gathering on my lower back and between my breasts. My hands shake in their clumsy gloves. I'm going to die out here. "What about short distances?" I hazard, grasping at final straws, at impossibilities.

Affirmative. The communications array could be reconfigured to allow short-range communication. However, the chance of anyone receiving your communication would be an infinitesimally small number. Almost zero.

"But it's possible."

Affirmative.

Then I'll do it. I have to. It's the only way I'm going to stave off the looming certainty of my death. I need to be busy. I need to try. "Talk me through it, *Pioneer*."

She does. With the clear instructions only a computer could manage, she tells me which tools to use and where they're located on my suit's belt. She explains how to open up the belly of the array to reveal its living wires, where to reroute them, and how to do it all as efficiently as possible with as little chance for a fuck-up.

I follow each instruction, one after the other, until I'm soaking with sweat — even my high-tech suit can't absorb the moisture I'm putting out — and after what feels like an eternity, I'm finished. The array is fixed, Frankensteined into a semi-useful version of itself.

"*Pioneer*," I say, putting away my tools, "put out a universal distress call. I'm going to look at the fuel tank hull breach."

Negative, says *Pioneer*. **You only have ten minutes of oxygen left.**

"It won't take me ten minutes," I insist. I don't voice the second part of my thought, which is: *I just want to look*. There's no way I'm fixing a hull breach, let alone in that short a time. But the comms array's sawed off edge is a sickness in my gut, a painful eyelash in my eye that won't budge. Someone... *something*... did that.

I swallow a bead of terror that threatens its way up my throat. I need to know.

So I pull myself hand over hand along the ship, my stomach in knots. I feel the vastness at my back like a loving nightmare, tendrils of it wrapping around my ankles and throat until I'm inevitably lost to it. I keep imagining the cosmos wrenching me off the ship, dragging me deep into itself, and I am a prisoner there forever, eyes wide, my screams soundless in the vacuum.

When I get to the fuel reserves, I see the breach immediately. It's not the jagged pockmark of a meteoroid or space debris. A panel of the hull is missing. It's a square of black against the ship's dull white, too precise to have been an accident of nature. Someone removed this panel.

I don't get any closer; I don't go to inspect it. I don't want to see the same ridges I saw on the comms array, the evidence of a saw that cut through it with precision.

I can't get back inside *Pioneer* fast enough. I yank myself along the tether. My mind makes up stories, envisions horrors. What if the thing that cut the comms, the monster that opened our fuel tank, is still here? What if it's clinging to the ship from the outside like some horrible lamprey, watching me?

By the time I get back to the airlock, my heart threatens to seize, my stomach to purge itself. I pull the slack of my tether inside, wrenching the outer door closed. The door moves slowly, painfully so, and I imagine hands curled around it from the outside. Long, pale, inhuman fingers, reaching and probing.

Finally, the airlock closes. I lock it, check that it's sealed at the control panel, and slam my thumb on the repressurization button. There's a whoosh and a fizz as air fills the room, and I steady myself as the false grav kicks in. As soon as the display turns green — pressurized — I whip off my helmet. I'm drenched in sweat; my hair clings to the sides of my face like wet threads. I unzip and unbutton myself, scrambling desperately out of my suit as if it's somehow contaminated.

When I'm free, I leave it there on the ground like the shed skin of a firmamental creature. I'm too shaken to hang it up properly, and I won't be going out again. I can't.

"*Pioneer*," I say, my voice so weak and shaky it's almost embarrassing, "is there anything... alive? Out there?"

I almost fall apart in the moment of silence before she responds.

`Negative.`

Part of me doesn't believe her. What if our idea of biological life is utterly foreign to what's out here, systems away? What we understand of the universe is so small, so pathetically minor, that it's almost laughable. It's *laughable* that we brought these tiny instruments, this breakable ship, these fallible scientists, all the way out here looking for life when our only frame of reference for "life" is what's on Earth. Our knowledge is so minute, a tiny droplet in a vast sea that never ends, and we had the audacity to think we knew what we were getting into.

3

I DON'T KNOW how long I've been sitting just outside the airlock, arms curled around my knees, a perfect re-enactment of my earlier breakdown. It's just that my limbs refuse to work, and my mind is not my friend just now. It's awash with everything wrong, nightmarish, half-seen, and shadowy. I don't trust myself.

An alert sounds. A soft, cloying chime. Different than the other alarm, but no less shocking in this awful silence.

`Proximity alert`, says *Pioneer*.

I lift my head. I must have heard wrong. "What?"

`Proximity alert.`

The alarm chimes. I remember it from training. It was supposed to be a good thing, an indication that we were nearing a planet, or an alien ship, that we were doing our jobs right. It doesn't feel like that now.

A slow spike of terror slices from the back of my throat down to my tailbone. I refuse to stand up, to move to the cockpit, to look out the viewscreen. "Proximity to what?"

`Unknown.`

I allow anger and frustration to take over, more manageable emotions than fear. "What do you mean, unknown?" And I'm finally standing, pushing sweat-thick hair out of my face, tucking it behind my ears. "What's out there? An asteroid? A ship?"

`Unknown. Negative. Unknown.`

I growl in frustration, a guttural sound that scrapes my throat. I don't want to see whatever it is with my own eyes. I don't want to know. I want *Pioneer* to tell me. "I didn't realize how *useless* you'd be out here," I spit, directing my fear and anger at the ship, who can't be hurt by it.

Pioneer says nothing.

"Unknown," I repeat acidly, dragging myself up the ladder to the cockpit. "Negative. Unknown."

A surge of relief fills me when I stare out the panoramic-viewscreen of the cockpit and see nothing but an infinity of stars. Maybe our sensors are malfunctioning; maybe it's a mistake. I'm about to say so to *Pioneer*, and then I see it:

An absence.

A space where the stars aren't, a shape of blackness. A shadow.

"*Pioneer*, what is that?" My voice is high-pitched. I lean forward, peering at the viewscreen. I see nothing, just the absence of *something*, like a cloud blocking the stars, a shape that moves slowly, swallowing up the distant pricks of light as it drifts blackly. And it's getting bigger; it's getting closer.

`Unknown.`

"You put out the distress call," I say, and it's not a question.

`Affirmative.`

"Um." My teeth chatter comically. Every muscle in my body is tense, my sweat now dry and caked to my frigid skin. My fingers shake when I pull up displays: infrared, sonar, radar, everything. All I get back is garbled nonsense, as if the ship refuses to understand whatever it's claiming is proximal to it. I grit my teeth. As frightened as I am, this could be a response to the distress call. This could be my salvation.

"S-send a message, *Pioneer*. I mean, hail them. I mean, send the welcome package."

`Affirmative`, says *Pioneer*.

My heart swells in my throat.

The "welcome package" is our way of introducing potential alien life to humanity, to Earth. It was designed to be a communique in every human language, plus binary and a celestial language that I insisted on including — the language of the stars. It's a primer on who we are, and what we're doing so far from home. That we're not a threat. We only want to be *friends*.

`Welcome package sent`, says *Pioneer*.

I wait. I don't know what for. There's no visible ship out there. Just a blackness, inching closer, threatening to swallow me. Shifting terror roils in my gut like a wraith. Whatever cut the comms array, the fuel tank — what if *this* is it? Some unknowable being, drifting darkly through the stars? What if it swallows me up, the whole ship, the dead crew? What if this shadow is the vacuum itself, the cosmos, coming to put an end to our human foolishness?

Something beeps on the dash. It's the comms display. I stare, open-mouthed.

After a moment, *Pioneer* says, `Ms. Selwyn, we are being hailed.`

I don't believe it. I see it, but I don't believe it. I see the flashing light. I hear what *Pioneer* tells me. But — it's nonsense. Ridiculous. Is the black shape, the shadow, trying to communicate with me?

Well, *someone* is.

I press a button, and there's a crackle: The sound of a channel opening.

I'm supposed to speak. I even wrote the script we're meant to use, once we learn how the alien life, or... whatever it is, prefers to communicate. It's a flow chart. A step-by-step method for introducing ourselves to the universe.

But I don't remember any of it just now.

So I wait.

And then, what feels like a million moments later, a voice comes through. It's muffled, breaking up — probably due to the damaged comms array — but I *understand* it.

"We've received your distress call," says the voice, deep and masculine. "Please confirm your status."

My knees threaten to give out, and I sit.

"*Pioneer*," I whisper. "Is he speaking English?"

`Affirmative.`

"I am," says the voice. "I got your welcome package. I learned it. I understand the primary language of your crew is English."

This is beyond anything we learned in training. There is no step on my flow chart that says, "In the event that the alien subject speaks fluent English, proceed to item 3F." Something in my chest ignites at the slow realization: I'm talking to an alien being. A lifeform, ostensibly. Someone with the ability to learn English in... was it only a matter of seconds? An entire *language*. My thoughts stutter and stop, as if my wiring is malfunctioning.

"Who..." I begin, then clear my throat, which has gone bone-dry. "Who are you?"

There's a beat of silence, cut through only by the crackle of the open channel.

"My name is Dorian Gray."

What the hell? "That's an Earth name," I manage.

"I picked it from one of the books in your welcome package."

"Oh. Of course." As if it's normal, a standard thing. *Of course* he did. Of course he dug through the entire library of Earth's works and landed on Oscar Wilde.

"You may call me what you like," says the voice that belongs to Dorian Gray. "I'm not sure you'd be able to pronounce my true name."

"What is it?" I ask, unable to stop myself, eager to hear his language. I find myself leaning forward to the view screen, as if this unseen creature's name alone can save me.

And then... he speaks. At least, I think it's speech. It almost *feels* like something, as if the deep and guttural utterance is drifting in from the speakers on the dash, into my ears and coating my brain in a syrupy, languid vibration.

Then the sensation is gone, and I gasp at the sudden absence. "That's your name?"

"Yes," says Dorian. "Apologies, if it felt strange. My language can be... detrimental, to some. It is not the same as yours."

Detrimental?

"No kidding," I breathe.

"Do you require assistance?"

"Yes." There's no reason to be coy. I've already sent the distress call and the welcome package. Either I accept his help, or I resign myself to death and join my crew in the dark eternity. "Are you..." I start, not knowing how to phrase it. "That shadow, blotting out the stars. Is it your ship?"

"It is," says Dorian. He sounds almost apologetic. But the words soothe me, and I wonder how he's managed to sound so *human*. There is nothing alien in the way he talks. He even, I realize, has an English accent. Southern English, to be precise — and posh.

"What assistance do you require?" Dorian asks.

"My comms array is broken," I respond, as if everything is fine, and normal, and this is a routine conversation. "I only managed to fix it enough for short-range transmissions. And I'm out of fuel. And..." I swallow. A razor-sharp pain shoots across my chest. "My crew is dead."

There's a pause on the other end of the line, as if Dorian is contemplating what I've said. Maybe he's deciding whether or not to nuke me. How can I possibly know? I've revealed all my weak spots — though I'm sure he must have already seen, must know that I'm truly stranded. That he could do as he wanted with my ship, with me, and I'd have no way of retaliating. *Pioneer* isn't a ship of war.

"Dead?" he says at last, his tone subdued.

"We traveled in stasis," I explain, trying not to let grief overwhelm me. "It's supposed to be safe, but... it wasn't. Their pods either malfunctioned, or their bodies couldn't take the extended coma. I'm the only one who woke up."

"I'm sorry to hear that."

"It's fine," I lie. His words, strange as they are coming from his inkblot of a ship, threaten to undo the weak threads that are holding me together. I cling to the saving grace that is Dorian, this being of shadows, the very thing we came here to find. Alien life. Maybe the mission hasn't failed. Not yet.

"I'd love to talk to you," I say awkwardly. "I mean, if you read the welcome packet, you know why we're out here. If you're willing, I'd like to..."

"You'd like to study me?"

I swallow. *Study* makes it sound detached, invasive. But he's not wrong. "Yes, technically, I'd be studying you. But you can study me back. And if you have the time, maybe you can help me fix my ship?"

This all sounds ridiculous, so much simpler and *less* than what's happening. Than what I'm feeling.

"Of course," he responds, unhesitating. "I'd love to let you study me. And I can help you with your ship."

My stomach twists. I'm not sure if it's fear or excitement. "That's... that would be great. Thank you."

"Do you have enough fuel to dock?"

I check the fuel display, and my heart sinks. "Not really. If I start the engines, they'll eat up most of what I have left just warming up. I'm dead in the water."

"Dead in the water," says Dorian, parroting me with a thoughtful tone. "Not to worry. I'll bring you in. But you'll need to strap yourself to something."

This is ominous in a vaguely comical way — *make sure you're sitting down for this*. In a suspended state of disbelief, I pull the cockpit chair's safety harness around me. I fasten it on either side. I'm as strapped in as a woman can get. "Done."

"Engaging now," he says.

There's a pause, a moment where I'm frozen in time and all of this is a spectacular dream, and then there's a horrible lurch, and I'm thrown side to side in the chair. My restraints keep me from injury, but it's not comfortable. I glance down at the navigation display, then through the viewscreen. We're moving. *Pioneer* is moving. And I've lost sight of Dorian's horrible invisible ship.

`Warning`, says *Pioneer*. `Unplanned inertial change.` A new alarm begins to blare.

"Sorry, *Pioneer*, I should have warned you," I bite out, fingers white-knuckled on my armrests. "We're being towed somehow. A tractor beam?"

"Something like that," says Dorian.

I start at the sound. I had forgotten the line was still open. "Is your ship shielded?" I ask.

"It is not shielded."

"Why can't I see it?"

"Your ship's computer does not understand it. *You* would not understand it."

"That's a big assumption."

"I read your welcome packet," says Dorian. "It's not an insult."

The process doesn't take long. It's strange — I felt the jolt as we were caught in Dorian's ship's *tractor beam* or whatever it is, and then nothing. Though I can see the stars moving as my ship turns, and then gradually, almost like lights winking out from a great distance, the stars go dark.

"*Pioneer*," I say, "status update?"

Unknown.

It's as if we were swallowed whole by darkness, enveloped in a velvet shroud.

"You're in my ship," says Dorian. "You may safely disembark."

4

I DON'T KNOW what I was expecting, but it wasn't this. When I disembark from *Pioneer*, I'm only wearing my standard-issue jumpsuit and boots, and am carrying a knapsack of essentials. Dorian assured me his ship's air is breathable for humans.

Still, it takes me a minute to orient myself. I'm standing in what looks like a massive cargo bay, big enough to hold five more *Pioneers*. And it's utterly empty, but for a stack of metal crates in the far corner. I'm alone.

Turning, I glance back at *Pioneer*. She seems so small from here, engulfed by the vast room. And beyond her, there's an enormous window that opens into space. Light refracts and wavers at the edges — probably some kind of forcefield, keeping the pressure intact. Beyond, the stars wink in the black like distant warnings. It sends shivers up the back of my neck. I never used to feel that way about the stars.

"This ship doesn't look *that* strange," I murmur aloud, remembering Dorian's words. "What's not to understand?"

"It's practically unfathomable mathematics and physics," a voice says, just behind me.

I spin to face him, pulse stuttering. I didn't hear him approach, but here he is, right in front of me. And he's *human*. The inexplicable urge to laugh bubbles in my chest, as if seeing the first living human since leaving Earth has made me insane with relief.

But as quickly as it came, the relief curdles and sours. Dorian is not human; I know that. He only... he *looks* so...

"You're confused about my appearance," he says.

Yes. Confused, but... something else. Something deeper, a coiling snake of sensation in my chest. My skin hums with the sense of uncanny familiarity. What is he?

Dorian Gray is beautiful. There is no other word for him. Handsome isn't enough, and somehow it's almost too tame a brush with which to paint him. He's beautiful but twisted, a human made with the painstaking strokes of an artist who's never seen one before: too-high cheekbones, a perfectly formed aristocratic nose, eyes heavy-lidded and ink-black. Night-dark hair frames a pale face, falling in loose waves to brush the top of his high starched collar. He's dressed like an ancient Victorian-era lordling, a bizarre image in that barren cargo bay. He stands statue-still.

I should be terrified of him, of what he isn't. I heard his true voice, felt it tonguing my brain. But my body isn't reacting in the way it should. My heart slams against my ribs, but not with fear.

"I thought it would put you at ease," he says, "if I assumed a human form."

"I'm not exactly sure I'm *at ease*."

"Would you prefer a different sort of human?" he asks, and his lip curls in a slight smirk.

Is he joking with me? Is he coming onto me? I grip the straps of my knapsack and try not to giggle. This is insane. Absolutely batshit insane. "This one's fine," I say, my mouth dry. I like this one fine. "But how do you do that?"

He shrugs; a human gesture. How has he learned us so quickly? "My ship is emitting a frequency that intercepts your brain's visual pathways. What your brain tells you you're seeing is not what is actually in front of you."

"Jesus."

"I won't hurt you."

"That's not my biggest worry right now."

"What is?"

Everything *else*, I want to say. My dead crew. My broken ship. Whatever broke said ship. But I'm only human, and I can't continue like this — talking to him, acting as if things are fine. I need a minute. "I'm... a little overwhelmed," I admit. "In shock, I think. And I just woke up from stasis. I'm not at my mental or physical best. All of this is... a lot."

"You need to rest." He studies me, his black eyes shining, snake-like. "Alone."

I nod. It occurs to me I'm probably somewhere past the point of shock by now, if there is such a thing. Lily would have known how the human brain reacts to things like this. Or maybe this *is* the reaction, I think, a shiver jumping up my spine. Maybe I'm still on the *Pioneer*, crouched outside the airlock, and this is my mind's way of inventing a savior.

Dorian moves then, a graceful drift toward me as if his legs and feet are only there for appearances' sake. He *is* walking. But there are no imperfections, no tics that come with growing up in a human body, no favored legs or crooked smiles. He is too perfect.

My skin crawls.

He extends a hand. "May I?"

I don't know what he wants. Is he asking to hold my hand? My knapsack? I shake my head, lips pressed together like a sullen child. I'm afraid I'm going to throw up. I've forgotten all the mission protocols. My brain isn't recalling what it should, and I'm ashamed. Just because I'm alone doesn't mean the mission is over, that I shouldn't be working. But here I am, confused and useless.

Dorian blinks, long lashes brushing ivory cheeks. "You need to come with me. I'm taking you to a room where you can rest, and be alone, until you are ready to speak with me. If you need to stop along the way, let me know. May I?"

I stare up at him, helpless. Our gazes meet, and my stomach twists. There are no pupils in his eyes that I can see — his irises are dark, inky black. A small mistake, but it's another thing that renders him so deeply alien that I am enthralled.

He holds my gaze like a fly in a web. "I promise, this form will be far less distressing than my true one."

"I'm not worried about your... *form*," I say. "It's just that you're not human. This isn't... I mean, I was *trained* for this, but..." But *what*? I'm in over my head? I forgot what to do and I'm scared of fucking up somehow? I should never have put myself forward for this mission?

"Ami," he says, my name supplicant on his lips. "I would never hurt you."

Tears prick the corners of my eyes, and I feel like I'm

outside the ship again, tethered but drifting, cocooned in the drape of space.

"You know my name," I murmur. My mind can't contain this. Contain him. I blink, hard.

Lily would have loved this. I would have loved this if I wasn't alone. If the ship wasn't damaged, if everything was as it should have been. If I wasn't *alone*.

"Of course," he says, softly. "I read your welcome package."

I nod, dropping my gaze to the floor. Right. He doesn't read minds; he isn't a wraith or a sorcerer. The ship is emitting a frequency. Centering myself, I focus my gaze on the floor. It's textured metal. And on my boots, scuffed leather. Their laces, thick and brown. I slowly inhale, filling my lungs. As I exhale through my nose, I remind myself of the most important truth: This is why I came. The mission hasn't failed. I can still do this, even alone.

When I raise my eyes to Dorian again, he's half smiling. My pulse flutters and I hate myself for it. "Okay," I say. "Lead the way."

The corridor he leads me through is like the docking bay — a generic spacefaring vessel interior, overlarge, drably structured, and empty. My footsteps echo, rubber on metal. It even sounds the way it should. But is this how the ship truly looks? Am I walking through a hall of smoke and mirrors?

"Where's the rest of your crew?" I ask when the repetitive echo of our footfalls becomes unbearable.

Dorian glances back at me, a line forming between heavy brows, an all-too-human expression. "I have no crew. I'm alone."

"But this ship is huge. How do you fly it?"

His mouth quirks. "She flies herself. The tech is very different from yours."

"Aren't you lonely?" The question slips out before I can stop it. What business is it of mine if he's lonely?

"Sometimes," he says, surprising me. "I've been out here for a long time. But I am often sleeping."

The words sound heavy in his mouth.

"Sleeping as in stasis?" I ask.

He shakes his head, strands of black hair shifting against his collar at the movement. "My kind doesn't need stasis. We can sleep very deeply for long periods of time, without food or water."

I'm fascinated, despite myself. "Do you age while you sleep?"

He darts a playful look over his shoulder. "Are you asking how old I am?"

My face heats, and I pray he doesn't understand what that means, that I'm embarrassed. But of course — he read the welcome packet. He's just as likely to be able to read every one of my tics, every facial expression, as if they were a book. "Actually," I admit, "if it's not rude..."

"My kind don't keep track of age like yours does. We live far too long for that."

"Oh. So... you're saying you're old."

He chuckles. "Very."

"Are we talking centuries or millennia here? In Earth years." I can't help myself, the questions keep coming, like I'm a human toddler meeting a real-life fireman for the first time.

He pauses, and I nearly walk into him, stopping short,

my nose inches from one of his shoulder blades. Then, in a low tone, he says, "Millennia."

I want to ask how long he's been on this ship, why he's all alone, and a million other questions. But his shoulders are tighter, his gait more matter-of-fact. I get the sense he's done talking.

As we make our way through the ship, taking seemingly random turns here and there, I lose all sense of how long we've been walking, how far from the cargo bay we are. For all I know, we're going in circles.

And in the absence of conversation, I begin to notice a strange sound. More like a vibration, a hum. As I focus on the sound, it gets louder. It starts under my ear at the jawbone, like a sour taste, and spiderwebs across my skull until I'm filled with it. It almost feels like tinnitus, or the ringing in your ear after a loud concert.

But this is different, more intense.

"What's that sound?" I finally ask, on edge.

"What sound?"

"The deep vibration. It sounds like a faraway engine. Is it the ship?"

Dorian glances back at me, and for an instant, I think I see a reflection in his black eyes, swirls of red like tiny nebulae. "I hear no sound."

When at last we come to a stop, I'm disoriented, as if I've been dreaming. At first, I don't understand why we're standing still. And then I see the door. It's the first proper door I've seen in Dorian's ship, which has been nothing but twisty corridors, angular high ceilings, and blank walls. The door is plain, as if cut into the ship wall. I see no knob, no button, no handle. No way to open it.

The air shifts, like a gust of wind in another world saw fit to visit this one, blurring the edges of what's before me. And then, without any prompting from me or Dorian, the door swings open.

"This is your room," he says. "It's not much, but I hope you'll find it comfortable."

He stands to one side, waiting for me to go in. It's dark; I can't see anything beyond a few shadowy shapes. Some part of me wants to refuse it, to say, *Actually, you know what, I'd rather stay on my own ship if it's all the same to you.* But it's a very distant, small part of me, and I quickly nudge it to the back of my mind. I don't want to be back on that coffin of a ship, familiar as it is.

My chest flutters with fear, anticipation, and even a little excitement.

Holding my breath, I move past Dorian into the room. *My* room on an alien spaceship.

A light flickers on, a warm orange glow. I exhale slowly, taking it in, and realize it's not a bad room. In fact, it's strangely normal. There's a bed on one side, partially ensconced in the wall; and on the other side is a table, a sink, and what looks like a fold-out privy. There's even a synthetic potted plant on the table. It's not unlike our bunks on *Pioneer*, if they were three times as big.

"The plant," I say, catching at my thoughts as if they're escaping wisps of smoke. I glance back at him. "It's a nice touch."

Dorian smiles from the doorway. He's leaning casually, one shoulder against the door frame, arms crossed. As if he's utterly human and always has been. "I like greenery."

"It's a pothos. An Earth plant."

"I know." His smile widens. "I read the welcome package. A pothos requires low light, infrequent watering, and makes for a hearty house plant. But you're tired, overwhelmed. I'll leave you now."

"Wait." I blurt it out, his words sinking in. My hands prickle and I drop my knapsack, letting it thump to the ground. "It's real?"

Before Dorian can answer, I'm bending over the plant, gingerly pressing fingers to its waxy leaves. I breathe deeply. There's soil in the pot. It's *real*. It smells like Earth, and it fills me with an undefinable ache, of grief or of relief, and I choke back tears.

Then I freeze, remembering what Dorian said about the ship, the frequency. I spin towards him. He's watching me with an almost overwhelming intensity, his unblinking black eyes framed by unnaturally long lashes, head tilted down slightly, as if he's starving and I'm a meal. But he blinks, his muscles relax, and he's human again.

Well... as human as he'll ever be.

I'm already going mad in this place.

"It's just an illusion," I accuse him. "Not a real plant at all."

"Your fingers touched it," he says, black eyes shining. "You smelled it. The touch and smell pathways in your brain recognized it as a living thing. Does that not make it real?"

This is basic stuff. Stoner Thoughts 101. I've heard it all before in my early twenties, passing a joint with friends, staring up at the sky, and wondering what it all meant. We were naive, sweet things who thought we'd make something of the world, be remembered, put our own notches in the ribbon of time.

Dorian hovers inside the door for a moment. "I'll leave you now," he says again.

I'm taken by a wild urge to ask him not to. *Stay*, I want to plead. *Don't leave me alone.* His presence should be more unsettling than it is, more foreign, more frightening. But it's not. He feels, against all reason, like a comfort.

"If you need me," he says, backing out of the room, "all you have to do is call my name."

Then the door closes, clicking shut, and I'm alone in this room that was made just for me. A simulacrum of quietude. I want to stay awake, I want to inspect every corner, take readings and make notes. I've brought tools with me, and tech. But I realize suddenly how tired I am, so tired that my body seems to be on the verge of collapse.

I sit on the bed, untie my boots, and kick them off. I lie down, jumpsuit still on. But there's no way I'm sleeping here, no matter how exhausted I am. I'll probably lie in bed for ages, wide awake with newness and agitation, every sound and thought pattering at my brain like uneasy footsteps. I stare up at the ceiling, that distant hum pressing like a heavy weight on my thoughts. And then the reality of the ship itself, the heaviness of my grief and overwhelm, the existence of Dorian, join the hum and press down on my thoughts and smother them, until unconsciousness laps over me like dark waters.

5

I WAKE IN THE DARK. The light has turned off, though the room isn't totally black. There's a viewscreen on the far side of the room, glowing. I didn't notice it before, or maybe it wasn't turned on. It shows the void of space, dotted with pinpricks of light, and a brighter red glow that might be a planet or a red giant.

A slow trickle of unease crawls up my spine. My body feels weightless and untethered in this half-sleep, as if in pushing back my blankets, I'll drift up and out, through the viewscreen, into the abyss.

I look quickly away from the stars.

And I see it there — a towering black shape in the corner. Watching me. His eyes catch the false starlight and glint like ghostly orbs. *Dorian*.

I sit up, adrenaline streaking through my veins. The light flickers on at my movement, and I blink in the brightness. He's gone.

I glance around to find the room empty, except for my

labored breaths and the pothos, and my knapsack on the floor.

In that soft orange light, I feel silly.

"You're fine, Ami," I say aloud, but the tone is unconvincing, my voice thick and quavering. I swallow. "It was a shadow. A sleep paralysis demon, at worst."

My nervous system believes otherwise.

I can't try to sleep again; I don't want to see another shadow in the corner. With a grunt, I drag my knapsack up onto the bed, methodically removing its contents. I lay them out before me on the blanket: a set of tools, a handheld comm unit, a fresh change of clothes, a half dozen nutrient bars, a liter of water, a basic survival kit, a first aid kit, and a battered copy of *Contact*. The essentials.

One by one, I check my tools, the kits, and my comm unit. They're all intact, just as I packed them. I flip through the book — why, I don't know, only that it comforts me, and seeing the words laid out exactly as they should be, exactly as I've read them countless times before, slows the racing of my pulse.

It's supposed to be life-changing, I remind myself. This meeting. This first contact. It's what I'm here for, what I've dreamed of for so, so long. It's what *humanity* has dreamed of. I'm living it.

I unwrap one of the nutrient bars and eat it slowly. My gut complains. I realize I haven't eaten since before stasis sleep. I haven't eaten in *years*. I would kill for the hot bitter taste of coffee, but my adrenaline has done a fine job of waking me.

When I finish the nutrient bar, I pull on my boots. There's no way I'm calling for Dorian right now; I don't want him to see what a jumpy neurotic I'm becoming. But there's even less of a chance that I'll stay in this room like I'm some kind of prisoner. I'm beginning to worry in a paranoid, anxious way that that's exactly what I am — a mouse in a cage, about to be let loose in some deep-space maze.

Approaching the door, a lance of fear cuts through me. This is the moment of truth. Will it open, or am I trapped? For a moment, nothing happens. And then as I inch closer to the door, there's a soft click, and it swings open. Relief floods me.

But a breath later, my shoulders tighten, and I hesitate. This might be another trick, an illusion. Nothing I see here is true. Dorian said it himself.

On some desperate, lonely impulse, I go back and grab the pothos, holding it in my arms like a blessed relic.

And then I step into the corridor.

I half expect Dorian to appear out of thin air, his umbral eyes boring into me. But I'm alone, and the vast corridor sweeps out to either side. I pick a direction and begin to walk. I've only gone a dozen paces or so when I come upon a door. It's just like the one to my room. My pulse speeds. Anything could be in there. Something I'm not meant to see, a secret of this illusory ship. I move to the door, and when I'm close enough, there's a click, and it swings open.

I nearly drop the pothos.

It *is* my room. There's my knapsack, on the bed. My book, my things laid out.

"What the fuck," I breathe. I know I didn't walk in a circle. I *know* it, but here I am, back in my room.

Glancing up and down the corridor with rising unease,

I clutch the pothos to my chest. If I walked in a straight line, I should be able to see the door I came out of. But I can't. There's nothing but a blank expanse of corridor, unmarked by windows or doors.

Fine. Okay. I must have turned around then, addled by lack of sleep and adrenaline.

Footsteps startle me from this frozen reverie, and I turn to see Dorian, inches from me. He hadn't been there a moment before. Had he? I blink, trying to remember. I was alone. I would have heard him coming. Despite my still-spiking fear, I'm struck by Dorian's appearance: his heavy-lidded eyes, gorgeous lips, that sculpted jaw. Not nearly as terrifying as the vision in the dark of my room, then. The shadows and my half-sleep had made him a monster, a towering specter in my mind. Right now he just looks like a man, a hair away from humanity.

His brows raise in polite concern.

I remember what he said when we met: *I promise, this form will be far less distressing than my true one.* But I don't find him distressing at all anymore, not like that. In the back of my mind I think I should be careful, keep my distance, but... the louder part of me says he's safe. He's good. I can see it in his eyes.

"Can I assist you with something?" he asks, like I'm a confused passenger on a commercial space flight.

"Sorry for disturbing you," I say, feeling sheepish for apologizing. But my gaze falls on the duplicate room, and a bead of fear trickles down my back. "I couldn't sleep. I tried to stretch my legs and take a walk, but... I looped back here again."

He glances at the door to my room, then back to me. I

can't read his expression. His skin is milky white like the moon. "The ship is trying to help you," he explains. "So that you don't get lost."

I scowl in confusion. "What?"

"The ship brought you back here, to your room. So you wouldn't get lost."

As if this explains everything. "How?"

He makes a face that's strangely disarming, almost boyishly impatient. "Do you want me to explain the physics of the process?"

"Yes." I'm being stubborn. I wouldn't understand the physics of the process if he wrote it out in the simplest of terms, but he doesn't have to know that.

He narrows his eyes and I almost suspect he's trying not to smile. "You're being stubborn."

My sharp intake of breath makes one of the pothos leaves shiver toward me, brushing my lip where I'm holding it close. "Are you reading my mind?"

"Don't be silly. I'm reading your body language. You want to be righteously angry with me because you're afraid of my ship." He crosses his arms, raising his eyebrows expectantly.

I'm speechless for a second, my eyes locked on his, my every emotion on full broadcast. He sees everything. "Right, okay," I admit. "But you should know that I saw..." I almost say *I saw you*, but I don't want him to think I'm completely off my rocker. The mission protocols come to me: *Maintain peaceful and professional communication at all costs. Never antagonize. Never present yourself as a threat.* "I saw something in my room, in the dark."

His black gaze holds me, and for a moment I feel that I

am a prisoner here, suspended in this endless corridor, a man who is not a man seeing into my soul, my organs, seeing and *seeing* until I am torn apart, atom by atom.

"You need more sleep," he says. "Real sleep, not stasis-sleep. Without a regular REM cycle, the human mind begins to fracture, blurring the line between reality and unreality. And my ship is... beyond your understanding. I told you that."

He *did* tell me that. I don't know what I expected. An admission? *Yes, I was lurking in your room, watching you sleep. Sorry.*

His face softens. "I won't hurt you, Ami. I told you that, too."

I want to feel safe here. I want this pulsating terror, the wash of paranoia in my veins, to stop. I want it so badly. But fight or flight has always been second nature to me. I spent my life trying not to fear the ones who were supposed to love me. I thought I'd left all that behind on Earth.

"Can I believe you?" The question is halting, vulnerable.

If Dorian is offended, he doesn't show it. "That's up to you."

"I want to. But your ship is..." I wrestle with myself, unsure how to put it without offending him, "really, um. *Unsettling*. No offense, but it feels kind of like a living nightmare."

I'm relieved when he laughs, a halting sound, as if he's never laughed before. "It's a side effect of the frequency," he says. "It's unsettling, your brain essentially lying to you. Eventually, when you're settled, you may be able to see the ship as it is. But I promise you, anything that seems strange, or unreal... it is only the ship attempting to protect you."

"Well, I don't like it," I say sullenly. But I relax despite myself. His laughter, the crinkles at the corners of his eyes, soothe me, even though I hate to admit it. He feels painfully human in this moment, and I am drawn to him, I need that connection. When did I last touch another person? When was I last embraced? *It's been years.*

I remember my brother sending me on my way, his face twisted as he wept, gripping me tightly and telling me he loved me. It was the first time he'd ever said it. My mother didn't bother to say goodbye. I don't think she cared that I was leaving forever. Maybe she was glad, relieved to be rid of the rebellious child, the daughter who made everything more difficult than it had to be. The daughter who should've been more like her brother: studious, patient, and contrite.

And I remember Lily, stroking my hair as I cried the night before we put ourselves in stasis, knowing we'd never see our families again. I didn't tell her that I wouldn't miss mine, other than Henry. It was Earth I was going to miss.

And I remember Mahdi, shaking everyone's hands as a farewell salute, a *See you on the other side*. And Vasilissa, rolling her eyes at him.

The last time I ever saw my crew alive.

"What is it you need?" Dorian asks.

My distress must be written across my face. I don't know where the urge comes from, but it's suddenly the most important thing in the world to me: "My crew," I say in a strangled voice. "They're still on *Pioneer*. I... I should hold a ceremony for them. A funeral, I guess."

"A funeral," echoes Dorian. "Are you all right?"

"Yeah, I just—"

"You don't have to lie," he says, and it's a kindness.

My chin trembles. "They were my friends. They should be here with me. I just want to say a few words. It's Earth custom to honor the dead." Little good it will do them.

"I read your welcome package," he says softly. "I understand."

We return to the docking bay. The walk isn't as strange or unending as it felt earlier. I realize I have no idea what time it is, and then I realize I don't care. We're in space. There's no sun to rise each morning, no moon drifting blue around us, no rising tide or cooling sands. Only darkness.

You need more sleep. Real sleep. Dorian's words curdle in my brain. How did he know I'd only just come out of stasis? Did he study the readouts on *Pioneer* while I was asleep in my room? Are his senses so sharp, so advanced, that he can tell how rested someone is just by looking at them? I pinch the bridge of my nose, squeezing my eyes closed for a second. Or maybe I already told him and forgot.

My anxious thoughts flee when we come to the docking bay, and I see *Pioneer* again. She's exactly as I remember, solid, an anchor. I would hug her if I could, wet her hull with desperate tears. Instead, I take a long, deep breath.

"How would you like to proceed?" Dorian asks, laying a shockingly warm hand on my shoulder. "Earth spacefaring tradition states we should—"

"Eject the bodies into space," I finish, trying not to lean into his touch. "I can't do that. I mean..." I struggle for the words. I'm not ready to let them go. I need them, and I need to find out what happened to them, so it doesn't happen to me when I return home... if I ever do. And I need them here. I don't want to be alone. "Not yet. I don't want to do that yet."

Dorian nods, squeezes my shoulder once, then lets his hand drop.

I feel bereft without his touch.

Shivering, I realize I'm supposed to be leading this memorial, this goodbye, whatever it is. But I don't know how. I feel it would be right to board *Pioneer* and see them again, to properly say farewell, but I don't want to. The ship has become their tomb. And while I'm deeply unsettled by Dorian's ship, the idea of crawling back inside *Pioneer*, closed inside her narrow vertical passages, makes me want to scream.

"I'll say it here." I crouch to set the pothos on the floor. This plant might be as close to Earth as I'll ever be again, illusion or not. Running my fingers over the leaves, I sigh. "I'm sorry, Mahdi. Lily. Vasilissa. I'm sorry you didn't make it. I wish..." No, wishing is for me, a selfish act. Instead, I recite the only poem I know by heart, a short verse by Gerard Manley Hopkins. "I have desired to go," I begin shakily, "where springs not fail, to fields where flies no sharp and sided hail... and a few lilies blow."

My throat burns, and I can't stop the tears from coming. I don't remember the rest of the poem, and I'm seconds away from crying uncontrollably. I take a few unsteady breaths, then stand, brushing away the stray wetness on my cheeks.

"May you rest peacefully," I choke out, holding back a sob.

I remember a funeral I attended once as a child. We sang "Amazing Grace," and dropped flowers onto the casket as it was lowered into the earth. Everyone was crying except for me. My pregnant mother clutched my arm with steely fingers, a silent flow of tears down her cheeks. I sometimes wonder if they were real, or if she had practiced crying for the occasion. Henry hadn't been born yet. He was lucky, not to know our dad. I remember that funeral as one of the best days of my life.

But I can't remember the words to "Amazing Grace."

My crew's souls will find the way home, I think. God, if he exists, is with them now. God won't abandon his children, no matter how far we stray from home.

I think I almost believe it.

I start crying at last. Sobs wrack my body, wild and uncontrolled like the wails of a desperate infant. I reach for the pothos as if its false leaves will grant me solace. And then hands are hooking under my armpits, pulling me up to my feet. Arms wrap around me, pulling me into a tight embrace. My face presses to Dorian's chest. He's warm, and I can feel his heartbeat. He smells like sweat and skin. *Human.*

I let him hold me while I cry, and for a moment, I pretend I'm not alone.

6

THE WORLD MELTS AWAY. I am not stranded in deep space, not the last surviving member of a doomed crew, not alone in the world. I'm held by the heat of him, the pulse of blood through veins, the judder of his breath as he inhales, ruffling my hair. And then comes the distant, enveloping, aural cocoon of that distant hum — permeating me from epidermis to aorta, reaching in with invisible fingers and holding me.

Holding me.

You're fine, Ami. The reminder doesn't come from me. It's not spoken aloud or even in the spark of unconscious thought. It's from elsewhere, outside of me, maybe even traversing the path of the hum that fills my thoughts.

You're fine.

I *am* fine. More than fine. My fear and anxiety seem to melt away as if they never were. Dorian has me.

His hand snakes up my back, feather-soft, hesitant, but flame-hot. I inhale sharply as his fingertips feather at my neck, then cup the nape. And then his fingers are buried in my hair, intimate and thrilling. I gasp but make no move to untangle myself from him. Why should I? His touch is comfort. His voice, delicate in my head, is a comfort.

Is it his voice, telling me I'm fine? Is he speaking to me subconsciously somehow, his words winding through my brain stem like a drug? The thought, vague as it is, brings me back to myself. I feel my body stiffen, as if from far away; as if I'm dreaming, and the alarm is beginning to blare, but I'm trapped in the cloudy unreal, the inescapable vision. But all of this *is* real. I am truly here, in the docking bay of Dorian's alien ship, and my crew is dead.

"I'm sorry," Dorian murmurs, halting, his voice muffled. He's buried his face in my hair. His breath is hot on my ear. "There was nothing I could do."

Like a pale light flickering on, a thought cuts through the fog: he's upset. Sad for me. Trying to comfort this soft human who drifted into his corner of space. But something in his voice betrays him — he didn't mean to say what he just did. Or perhaps he thought I wouldn't hear it.

He senses my hesitation, this moment of clarity, and his body stiffens.

Looking up at last to meet his gaze, I'm again struck by the blackness of his eyes, the depth and scope. It's like I'm looking out the viewscreen and into the universe, pricked with far-distant stars, none of which do anything to brighten the umbra. I'm both adrift and trapped like a rabbit by a fox. And he is the fox, shadowed in dusk.

"I know that," I murmur, my voice thick with weeping. "Of course there was nothing you could do."

He glances away, then back to me, and the power of his gaze has lessened. I'm released.

I breathe deep, and with the flood of oxygen to my lungs, my face no longer buried in Dorian, in the soft part of him where shoulder meets chest, discomfort crawls in my gut.

Not human. He's not human.

He waits as if to see if I'll bolt, or if I'll stay and let him continue to enfold me.

I should be afraid of him.

But I'm responding to him like a strange, unearthly drug. I want to know every inch of Dorian. Somehow he is an island in the storm-swept sea of my loneliness and grief.

"What are you?" I ask, and I realize that I'm clutching his shirt in white-knuckled fists, holding *him* hostage. Willing him to answer, as if anything he says will illuminate this nightmare ship, my broken comms array, the damaged fuel tank. My dead crew.

Patiently, almost sadly, he smiles down at me, his moon-pale face framed elegantly by soft, jet-black hair. None of it is real. A painting, a beautiful facade of a thing that is not from Earth. "The last of my kind."

An evasion. "But what *is* your kind?"

He hooks a finger under my chin, tipping me up to him like an offering, our gazes locked. My chest and heart are loud with flowing blood, as if my pulse is rushing all around me, threatening to drown us in red, red, red. His voice is little more than a whisper. "I'm whatever you want me to be, Ami."

The shiver down my spine is a humiliation, the sharp

ache between my legs a betrayal. I've just laid my friends to rest, left their corpses to lie untouched by the passage of time, zipped up and safely kept in their stasis pods like the preserved kings of ancient Earth. My hot face is tear-stained. My heart aches and aches.

And I am frightened, I tell myself. I should be. I *am*.

"You're safe," Dorian says, as if my skittering thoughts are plain as day to him.

"But what kind of... of being are you," I manage, his finger still under my chin, so utterly real I imagine I can feel the whorls of his fingerprint, the faint pulse of blood under his skin.

The corner of his mouth lifts, and the smile is so disarming, so un-alien, that I'm helpless to it. My body arches toward him ever so slightly. It occurs to me that I should have asked this question the minute I arrived on his ship. That I should have been taking lengthy notes since the moment I disembarked from *Pioneer*, learning his language, his physiology, his habits. I'm a scientist, and Dorian is the mission. But I've been so tired. So overwhelmed. So confused. It's as if a cloud has been hanging over me, obscuring reality through a viscous haze.

And now *he's* here, eliciting the exact wrong sorts of emotions. The wrong bodily responses.

With what feels like an impossible amount of mental strength, I take one step away from him. One step, but it's enough to separate us, for him to drop his hands, for his heat to stop enveloping me like I'm oil and he's flame.

He blinks — momentarily surprised, I think — and then his expression crumples, his brows coming together in remorse, his lips twisting. "You need more sleep," he says, backing away with one hasty step. The gulf between us feels unbearable. "I see it in your eyes, they're hazy with exhaustion. You're grieving."

I'm fine, I want to lie. *Come back*, I want to beg, even though I'm the one who moved away, who put this chasm between us. But he's right. I'm sleep-deprived, grieving. All I've eaten in who knows how long is one nutrient bar. I'm every kind of fucked up.

And he's an alien. I press the heel of one hand to my eye, savoring the dully painful burst of light and color.

"I'll take you back to your room," Dorian says, holding out a hand.

I want to take it, but I'm suddenly afraid that if I do, I'll never want to let go. Instead, I nod, shoving my hands into the pockets of my jumpsuit. He bends to pick up the pothos, holding it as if it's a priceless artifact, and he its steward.

I trail after Dorian and the pothos, back through the empty corridors, and I try to think of things I know: The gnarled tree outside my childhood window, the one I wasn't allowed to climb even though its branches were so thick and shaded with leaves in the summer. Lily's uneven teeth when she smiled, one front tooth just slightly overlapping the other, the smile she hated even though it softened her. Lying on the beach in a wet swimsuit, sand between my toes and stuck to patches of skin. The pop of a blackened candle wick, thick and fragrant smoke swirling upward on a rainy October evening. Fresh coffee in the morning, so hot it almost burns. The relief of the first night I spent in my own place, the month I turned eighteen, utterly broke but finally free.

By the time we return to my room, my mind is in another place altogether. In my head, I'm back home, and no one is dead, and I'm as close to happy as I ever got, on Earth.

7

I DREAM that I am falling. *Pioneer* grows ever smaller as I tumble away, my tether trailing out behind me. Her hull winks in the starlight until she is a speck of light, and then nothing at all. I'm falling and falling, though I can't feel the rush of air around me, or see the ground rush up to greet me. I feel nothing but the pull of unseen gravity. Infinite night surrounds me like smoke in water, pooling above my earlobes, wreathing itself in my hair. I'm wearing no helmet. I'm wearing nothing at all. The darkness, the swell of space, softly curls against me, covering me, snaking into my nose and my ears and finally my eyes, filling up the gaps between eyeball and skin, around into the socket, flowing into me until I'm full to burst. I'm blind. I'm in agony. I can't yell, or thrash to free myself. I'm frozen in place while the universe drowns me.

A choked cry wakes me, and I'm drenched in cold sweat. The bedclothes cling to clammy flesh. My hair sticks to my face. Coughing, I realize the strangled cry was my own.

"Jesus," I say, pulling damp sheets away from my bare legs, hating the feel of it. My underclothes are soaked through.

I mutter a quiet prayer of thanks to my foresight, rummaging in my knapsack for a fresh set. I toss the sweat-soiled pair to the other side of the small room, and I'm naked, shivering as my sweat dries in the chill air. I remember what I saw before, the last time I slept here. Dorian, or a shape like him, either real or imagined. A watching shadow.

My gut knotting sickeningly, my gaze darts to the far corner. And even though the lights are on and I'm awake, a horrible sensation takes hold of me. As if I almost saw, just for an instant... a flickering darkness. A black cloud vanishing.

It's late. I haven't slept properly in days. And I know that minds play tricks, even in the most familiar circumstances.

Just to make sure, because I'll never get back to sleep in this state, I go to the corner. I press my hand to the walls, look up at the ceiling, down to the floor. I even crouch on my hands and knees and prod at the floor as if there's a trapdoor there, like I'm sleeping in some Victorian-era hoax house. As if I've been lured in to watch a fake seance, only to discover that there are magnets in the table and I've been tricked by Pepper's ghost.

But there's no trapdoor, no mirrored glass, no vent from which a gust of air might burst and startle me.

I remember I'm naked, and hurry to pull on the clean pair of underclothes. A clean jumpsuit comes next, then socks. As I lace up my boots, I wish I knew how long I slept.

The viewscreen is ever-night, the slow passage of celestial bodies across a dark canvas.

This time, when I leave my room chewing the last of my nutrient bar, I hesitate outside the door. I have no idea what Dorian could be doing, how he spends his time when he's not comforting lost humans. Before he left me here, after the memorial, he said again, "Call for me if you need anything." But surely he can't hear me throughout the ship. Unless there's an acoustic design, like the ship is a cosmic whispering gallery.

I don't want to call for him. The memory of his hands on me, his breath on my ear, catches in my throat like a half-swallowed pill. But at the same time, I realize I'm dying to be near him. He's like an itch I can't scratch. I want to understand him. To know what sort of thing he is, what his true form might look like.

What I *do* know is that I can't trust myself around him.

The thought sits heavily in my stomach, setting me on edge. I try to shove it aside, letting loose a wretched sigh. I can't wander the ship alone; it will bring me in a loop again, back to my room.

"Dorian," I say, feeling oddly shy. Will he think I'm pathetic, hanging around my room until my host comes to lead me around like a lost puppy?

And then there are footsteps, and I turn to see Dorian.

He's wearing the same outfit as before, as if he fell from the worn cover of a Victorian novel. And I lose my breath for a moment at the sight of him, though I already know how he looks. His eyes are like the night, ever the same yet always changing, constellations wheeling across his visage like shining beacons.

"How did you get here so fast?" I ask. "I mean, did you walk here?"

He narrows his eyes, smiling thoughtfully. "I got here in my own way. How can I assist you, Ami?"

I frown. He won't answer *anything*. I wonder if it's deliberate, or whether he truly worries that my frail human mind can't grasp the concept of him. "I want to fix my comms array," I announce. "I brought my tools, but I may need materials. I can give you a list of what I'd need, if... if you happen to have any spare parts lying around."

It's a wild shot in the dark, but he doesn't immediately shut me down. Instead, shockingly, he nods. "I'll see what I can find."

My heart leaps. If I can fix the comms array, and the fuel tank, then maybe... but I don't let myself think that far ahead. I should operate as if I'm never going home. Then I ask, "Would you mind talking to me, while I work? I'd like to learn more about you. Not in an invasive way. I just... want to get to know you."

He smiles, his eyes glinting with understanding. "You want to study me."

"Get to *know* you."

He tilts his head, and I suddenly feel that I'm the one being studied, plastered to a petri dish and held up to a microscope. "We can do, or talk about, whatever you'd like, Ami."

I swallow dryly. "Okay, great."

"Ask me something."

"Now?"

He nods. "Anything."

"Right, well..." I consider all the thousands of questions

that have been clanging around in my head since I woke up from stasis. "Why did you pick Dorian Gray?"

"It was an interesting book."

I raise a brow. "You *read* it?"

His mouth twitches as if he's trying not to laugh. "It's not that long."

"Listen, I realize you went through the entire welcome package in record time. I mean, faster than any human could begin to compute all that information. And learned a language on top of that. But you also *read* the book?"

"Yes," he says. "I read them all."

If I were a cartoon, my jaw would be on the floor. He can't mean what I think he means. "Wait. All what?"

"All the books."

"By Oscar Wilde?"

"No, *all* the books. Every book in your welcome package. Earth's literary canon."

I splutter, momentarily lost for words. That's over half a million books.

"Why?" he asks, lips curling in a slow smile. "Do you find that impressive?"

I'm suddenly blushing, but I can't help it. I do. I find it *very* impressive. "Are you even biological?" I ask. "Are you an android?"

He laughs, the second time I've heard it, a halting, deep reverberation in his chest. I like the sound. It's warm and open. "No," he says. "I'm not an android. But I have a very complex brain. Earth neuroscientists would enjoy analyzing it."

"They fucking would," I agree, laughing a little despite myself.

"I liked Oscar Wilde the best," Dorian says. "Funny. Sad. Lovely prose. And I liked the name Dorian Gray."

"Is that why you're... dressed like that?" I ask, waving a hand at his cravat, crisp frock coat, starched high collar.

He visibly swallows and glances away. "No," he says. "Not quite."

How strange. I wish he'd open up and tell me everything, *everything*. I want to know more. I want him to lay himself bare to me. I want to chart his nervous system, count his lungfuls of air, unfurl his DNA one strand at a time. "Do you identify with Dorian Gray?"

He blinks, visibly surprised at the question. "Do you think I should?"

"I asked *you*."

"No," he answers. "I've never had a portrait done."

And then I'm laughing, and he joins me, and he leads the way to the docking bay, half a step ahead of me. We walk together, sharing space. But as we pass through the ship, the laughter fades into cold unease as I become distracted. Because with every step, I hear that distant sound more loudly. That hum, the engine's roar, the strange tinnitus of deep space, the thing Dorian doesn't hear.

But I say nothing. I don't want to admit to Dorian that I'm worried I might be going insane. It's not his problem. And Lily, whose problem it would have been as the crew's Psych expert, is gone.

I'm grateful for the potential distraction of repairing the comms array. It will give me something to do with my hands, and then... maybe then I'll feel better.

Keep telling yourself that, Ami.

Dorian leaves me alone in the docking bay, promising

to return with tools. I don't know where he'll get them, but I try not to dwell on the implications. I don't like thinking about the fact that everything around me, other than *Pioneer*, is not what it looks like.

The vast room seems to swell around me, the humming growing louder with it. I try to ignore how terrible I feel, how utterly isolated. I had known going into this mission, that I would be subjected to the strange and new, even bombarded by sensations and experiences that my brain might struggle to process. But the push and pull of fright and curiosity, of want and sharp-edged grief, threatens to wrench me apart on a molecular level.

And even as I shiver in the cold emptiness of that place, I ache to explore. I imagine the ship as if it's a sort of fluid thing, ever-changing, rooms moving and rearranging themselves, a labyrinth while I'm a hapless Theseus.

Who, then — or what — is the Minotaur?

8

THE LONGER I spend in the docking bay, its enormous maw opened up to the infinite cosmos, the louder my thoughts become. The louder that distant hum. It's unending. It has to be the ship's engine, no matter what Dorian said. Or some power supply, maybe even the flow of electricity through the ship's synthetic infrastructure, its metal and rubber veins, coppery filaments, its manufactured chassis. Dorian would be used to it by now. That's why he can't hear it.

Unsettled by the sound, my jaw tight and my shoulders drawn inward, I reach my limit. I don't know how much time has passed, but it feels as if I've been waiting for hours. And I realize I don't want to do this now; I don't want to occupy my hands and try to forget.

I want to talk to Dorian again. I want to laugh again, feel his warmth. He's my only anchor in this place, the only thing that keeps me afloat.

"Dorian," I say, almost a whisper in the echoing room. I'm afraid if I speak too loudly, the cosmos just outside the docking bay will hear me and suck me out through the forcefield and into itself, digesting me whole.

There's a hush of air against my neck, and Dorian is there.

I spin to face him, flushed. "You — you startled me," I snap, unable to keep the fear from my voice. My heart thunders.

His face falls, a perfect, loose wave of black falling over one eye as he lowers his chin deferentially. "I'm sorry."

I try to slow my breathing. "You didn't mean to. It's fine. Just... stop sneaking up on me like that."

"You called me."

"I know," I say, annoyed at myself for reacting. I open my mouth to explain that I was getting scared, that this docking bay fills with dread when he's not here with me, but I don't. Instead, I say, "I changed my mind. I don't want to work on my ship right now. I thought maybe we could... eat together? If you even eat, I mean. All I've had since waking up from stasis is nutrient bars."

"Anything you want." His stare bores into the tender flesh of my lip, where my teeth left their mark, and he's stone still like a gargoyle. I move away, ever so slightly. His gaze snaps up to mine. "Just tell me what you need."

The ship's hum pulses in my skull, like the reverberation of a strummed guitar string.

I'm seeing things that aren't there. Nothing here is real.

"I don't know what I need, Dorian."

He takes my hand in his, not waiting for permission. I remember the way he held me before, let me cry on him, let me break like a wave against him. I have felt this way before, in dreams. Where fear mixes with anticipation, and though the trees may bend in a gorgeous wind, the clouds may scud across a cerulean sky, a darkness lurks behind it all. A nightmare at the edges, its claws curving around the doorframe.

I have held men like this before and then fled. I've stayed, too. But were they different men, or was it always Dorian?

"Come with me," he says, and I am once again trailing after him, a puppet on a string.

By the time we reach our destination, I'm no longer stiff with fear. And the hum has lessened. I feel like I've woken from a dream or a long dissociation. Lily would have known. She could have explained it to me, why the brain shuts off and directs us elsewhere when reality becomes too much.

A trauma response, MiMi, I imagine her saying, her face all soft and sunlit. The way I'd prefer to remember her — not gray and lifeless, an empty shell.

Dorian ushers me into a room, his arm held out like a butler at a five-star hotel. I drift in, allowing my senses to take it in.

This is unlike any room I've ever seen. It's an ancient Victorian ballroom, and outside its tall windows, stars and nebulae wheel past. There is something wrong with the chandelier; it's tinged with red and appears to be suspended in midair. The floor feels uneven though it appears to be marble. At the center of the room sits a stately table set for two, and laden with food. Fruits and vegetables, loaves of bread, steaming tureens, and delicate iced cakes festoon the surface. It's a king's feast. I couldn't begin to make a dent in it.

"Where are we?" I ask, because it's the only reasonable question.

"The dining room," says Dorian. "I've designed it for you."

I turn to him, and he looks so painfully hopeful, almost eager. "Oh."

His face falls. "You don't like it."

"No, it's..." I falter. "It's beautiful. I'm just surprised. I've never eaten in a room like this."

He frowns. "I see."

I don't know where to begin explaining the ancient architecture, how Earth's 1800s occurred centuries and centuries before I was born, how there's no room left on the planet for even a house this big, let alone one dining room. So I don't. "It's *very* beautiful," I amend. "I mean, I've always wanted to visit this sort of place. Ancient homes, you know. The old, old things that no longer exist except in history books."

"You miss Earth," he says and moves toward me. "I can make other rooms for you, Ami. Other places. Show you things you've never seen before."

His eyes are swirling pools of everything I want. I let him wrap an arm around me, let him steer me toward the table. He pulls out a chair for me, and I sit. It's easy to let him do these things. To let him direct me. I'm exhausted, my emotional state hanging by a fraying thread. I don't *want* to take the lead. I want to let go.

He seats himself across from me, and we dine.

I don't know what I expected — that he might simply watch me eat, unable to consume human food, like some vampire, sipping a goblet of wine, waiting for his next victim to become drunk and willing. But he joins me, delicately chewing, shooting me wry smiles between sips of red wine. It's almost as if this is a normal meal. It's almost as if I'm not shaken to my core, never to recover.

"What do you really look like?" I ask, midway through a list of these sorts of questions: what do you call your kind (*You wouldn't comprehend the word, it's worse than my name*), where is your home planet (*Billions of light-years from here*), is it anything like Earth (*No*), how can you eat this food (*By putting it in my mouth and chewing*), what do you normally eat (*Nothing you'd recognize as food*), do you listen to music (*If the vibrations of the universe count as music, yes*). "I mean, *really*."

He leans back in his chair, pulling at the cravat at his throat. As it loosens, my gaze falls on his neck, his pulse. A smile curves one side of his mouth. "Think of it this way. You're looking at me, right now. And so what you see is how I look."

"But you're not human," I persist.

"I'm not," he agrees. "But it's the image I've chosen to project. If you touch me, I feel human. You know that."

My stomach flutters. "Show me your true form." I've had a little too much wine, so much that I'm conveniently not thinking about the fact that it's not real wine at all. I'm not thinking about how warm my face is, how Dorian's every glance is like a physical touch against shivering skin.

"I'd rather not."

"Please?"

"You wouldn't like it."

"You don't know that."

"You hardly seem to like *this* form."

"That's not true. It's just... too beautiful. I was trained for all kinds of biological oddities." I catch myself. "Not that you're an oddity. But the body you've chosen, it's... a lot."

He leans forward, chin resting on folded hands, elbows on the table. "How so?"

Heat rises in my face. I've driven myself into this corner. I take another swig of wine. "You're, well, I'm not sure if this will make sense, but you're my type."

I avoid his gaze, blushing painfully. I don't know why I said it. Why I'm flirting *back*.

"I read your welcome package," he says slowly, and his tone is tinged with unspent laughter. "I know what a *type* is."

"Oh?" I stare at the edge of my wine glass, running a shaking finger along the crystal until it makes a faint sound. "Well, with millions of options at your disposal, you picked exactly the kind of body, and strangely, exactly the kind of *clothes* that—" I stop myself, my breath hitching.

What am I *doing*? This is every kind of bizarre. I'm in a Victorian ballroom inside a vast alien ship, drinking wine with the alien himself.

"Exactly the kind of body that... what?" Dorian says, but it's clear that he knows exactly what.

Exactly the kind of body that makes me want to lose control.

But he knew that, didn't he? He tailored himself for me.

I stand abruptly, knocking my chair over. It clatters to the floor, the sound ringing ostentatiously in that quiet room. "Thank you for dinner." It's a rush of words, my heart pounding against my ribs.

Dorian watches me intently but says nothing.

"I'm sorry," I add. "I'm tired, and it's late. Or it feels late. I don't know what time... anyway, I should sleep."

He rises gracefully, showing no sign of disappointment or anger, any of the usual razor-sharp edges a man might show after a date cut short. The wine that isn't real feels sickly in my stomach. This isn't a date.

I take Dorian's offered arm as he escorts me back to my room. He's steady and firm, and for a second I pretend that he is just as human as I am. When we say goodnight, he is the perfect gentleman, without a single roving hand or salacious word.

And as the door closes behind me, leaving me alone once again, I press my hands to my face, nearly suffocating against my clammy palms. All the while, somewhere deep in the ship, I feel it at the core of me: that far-off hum.

9

THE NEXT MORNING, I take the stopwatch from my selection of knapsack tools and conduct an experiment. It's simple, probably pointless, but I need something to do. I can't call for Dorian, not after embarrassing myself last night. I had far too much wine and lost my stupid head. I'm lonely, but not *that* lonely.

So instead of asking him to bring me back to the docking bay to have a go at my comms array, I pace the corridor outside my room. I walk in one direction until I come to my room's door again. Confirmed: the ship is still looping. I make an exact count of steps, of the time it takes, of the breaths that leave my lungs as I go. If I can figure out how the hallway is looping, I can extrapolate for the rest of the ship. I'll be able to categorize this place. I'll make it real. I'll wrap my brain around it.

A dozen steps bring me from one door to the next, a complete loop. Opening it, I peer inside — it is my room, just as I left it. The pothos waits greenly in the corner, my knapsack sits hunched on the bed. My dirty clothes lie piled in the far corner.

Something slips past, behind me in the corridor.

I spin, heart in my throat. It was nothing but a hint of flickering shadow in my periphery, but my pulse beats a frantic staccato as I search wildly for what I thought I saw. But it's gone. There's nothing watching me, nothing hovering there waiting to strike. There are no undulating shadows, no glinting eyes. The corridor is empty.

Then why is my heart thudding, my gut in knots? Why does everything seem brighter, sharper, worse?

"You're fine," I mutter. But I'm bursting with adrenaline, and my fingers shake.

Stubbornly, I force myself to conduct three more experiments. I walk in a different direction, then both ways, backwards.

When I walk backwards, I can still see my original door when the new one appears beside me. I open it, and I'm in my room again. Does this mean there are multiple versions of my room, an endless array, lined up like a room buffet? Or am I somehow, without actually feeling it, wandering in circles? It's like I'm hooked up to a permanent virtual reality rig.

If my brain can't process the ship itself, there must be other things it isn't processing, not just Dorian. I know that as soon as an image hits the brain, it can be altered by gray matter, flipped and molded and enhanced as the mind sees fit. I am wandering in circles, circles, and circles, Theseus caught in a hamster's wheel.

Dorian.

The thought of him creeps up on me unwanted, his

smile, lips stained with red wine. His delicately long fingers in my hair. His laugh. His breath against my—

"Fuck *off*," I hiss, shaking my head, rejecting the thought.

I continue pacing. I'm glad to be distracting myself, though I acknowledge the experiment is achieving nothing. And I still can't shake the feeling that something is watching me, a slither of presence always *there* but never seen.

And always that humming in the distance.

A prickle runs up the back of my neck, and all of a sudden I don't want to be out here. The corridor is too vast and yet too small, I'm claustrophobic in this endless loop, and I want out. Stumbling in my haste, I dart into my room and slam the door behind me, wishing for a lock. Sweat pricks my upper lip, my palms.

"You. Are. Fine." The words shake but I'm adamant. I'm fine.

Like an overstimulated child, I lower myself to the floor and lie on my back, eyes closed, breathing hard and fast. The floor is cool, and I pretend I'm in the garden of my childhood best friend's house, where stepping stones wound through overgrown ferns and foxgloves, and bees hummed all summer long. I would go there sometimes, when my mother was feeling unusually generous, and I'd spend the night. There, I was safe. Just for a little bit, my mother couldn't touch me. The hush of imaginary wind brushes my cheek. I imagine late afternoon sunbeams alighting on my eyelids. I am seeing gold, thick like honey. I am safe.

My breathing begins to slow.

I open my eyes at last. The plain ceiling greets me, the orange glow of ambient lighting. I roll sideways, about to push myself up to my knees when I see it.

Something is wedged between the bedframe and the wall, only visible from down here. A piece of pink plastic. Probably something of mine, fallen down and forgotten, stuck here while I slept.

It takes me a moment to wiggle the thing free, and then with a grunt, it comes loose.

My heart stops.

It's a hair comb. The cheap kind you get at a drugstore, some brandless thing that will break within months of use. But it's not my comb. I don't even use combs — all I have to do is run my fingers through my fine black hair a few times, and it's done. But I *know* this comb.

It's Vasilissa's comb.

"What the fuck," I say like it's a prayer, turning the comb over and over in my hands.

I consider the possibilities: It is Vasilissa's comb, but in my grief-fueled shock I put it in my knapsack by mistake. It is *my* comb, and I forgot about it during stasis. It is not a comb at all, but some unidentified object that Dorian's ship has decided should look like Vasilissa's comb. Or it doesn't exist at all, and I'm hallucinating.

Thing is, I don't remember packing it. I don't remember removing it from my knapsack, let alone laying it out where it might fall and get stuck in the bed frame.

Am I going insane? I wonder, not for the first time, thumbing the plastic, pressing the pointed prongs into each of my fingers, one at a time. Or, worse, is Vasilissa's ghost haunting me? The prospect of ghosts, of revenge brought down upon me by my crewmates, turns my lungs to ice.

No, ghosts aren't real. This is a *comb*. I am in a spaceship that alters the way I perceive reality. Ghosts aren't real. And this is a comb.

A knock sounds at the door, a low and metallic thud. A scream catches in my throat, and I force it back down, embarrassed by this reaction. But my body is on the verge of panic, and my gullet pulls tight, my knees shake as I get to my feet. I shove the comb deep into my pocket. I open the door.

Dorian looms in the doorway, dark and tall and all-consuming. He regards me with a strange expression. "Are you all right?"

"Yes," I say, lying. Always lying. My teeth are on the verge of chattering, like some vintage Earth cartoon. In a minute I'll start stuttering, and my heart will beat out of my chest in a perfect shape, stretching the skin as it expands and contracts.

The shadows seem to watch me, every unseen terror, rigid and sitting up, like hares about to swarm or bolt. Dorian, too, watches me with intensity, and I avoid his eyes. I don't want him to see my fear there, or the comb.

"I was conducting some studies," I add. "Testing the corridors. Your ship won't let me go twelve paces beyond my room."

His brow furrows. "You're not a prisoner, if that's your worry. I thought you knew that."

I search for an adequate response and find none. I realize I'm picking at the skin around my thumbnail, picking and picking.

"I finally found the materials you need to fix your comms array," he says, tossing me a lifeline. "They're in the cargo bay. Would you like to—"

"Yes," I nearly shout, eager to get out of this room, this cyclical nightmare. Working on something, using my hands and my muscles, focusing on a project — that will calm me down. I'm sure of it. It has to.

He holds out a hand, an invitation, a welcome. None of which I should want. *I want it so much.* "Come."

I can't say no. I don't want to say no. So I follow him, hands in my pockets, the pink plastic comb held firmly in one fist until the prongs press into my skin, stinging. I cannot shake the feeling that I'm being watched, the ghosts of my crew or of this ship, shadowing me.

10

THE BROKEN COMMS array waits for me in the cargo bay. It rests on the floor, too large for the worktable just to the left of the door, its various parts sticking out at strange angles like a metallic carapace, a dead insect. There are tools laid out before it, a neat line of implements, exactly the ones I need.

For a moment, I am hopeful. A flicker of elation: the prospect of repair, of going home. Fixing *Pioneer*. Refueling her. And then...

And then?

My glimmer of hope judders and fades, and then it's gone. And then — what? Just go back to Earth, where everyone I once knew will be long dead? Then, what...? I write up a debrief about Dorian, say "thanks for everything," and continue the mission? I'm a woman with a ship and a dead crew. With ghosts clinging to my heels, tripping me up. A pink comb in my pocket that shouldn't exist. An alien man, whispering in my ear. A whisper I'm afraid won't ever let me go, no matter how far I flee.

"I trust this is what you need," says Dorian, and he is close, just behind my shoulder. His deep voice permeates my being.

With a barely contained shudder, I remember his true voice, its tonguing of my brain, and I swallow to keep the bile from rising. But I don't move away. I'm reeled in, a fish at the end of his line. I turn my head, chin rising, and he is so close, too close.

"Thank you," I manage, and drag myself to the comms array. I crouch before it, running a finger along the ridged edge where it was damaged. Whatever thing did this, whether alien or something worse, it lives at the edge of my thoughts. It's in the far corners of the docking bay. It's just behind me, reaching, long-fingered and dark-eyed.

"Do you need help?" Dorian asks, coming to crouch beside me. His voice is warm but it's countered by the unceasing hum in my skull, the vastness of the cosmos, my ever-present horror on this ship.

"No," I say automatically, but I can't stop the blood from pooling in my face, between my legs. He owns me, and I hate it. I think about his eyes, the way he sometimes freezes and stares like a jungle predator. I avoid his gaze. "Thank you. I think I'm all right for now."

He leaves me alone to work. I embrace the repetition, the focus of it. First, I cut and shape a sheet of metal to replace the one that's missing. Dorian has provided a worktable, saws, and welding gear. I revel in the spark and grind as I cut through steel, millimeter by millimeter, exerting measured control over this one thing. This is one thing that is mine, that is not — cannot be — obscured or changed. The array is the array, and this steel *is* steel.

It has to be.

When I'm finished with the saw, I turn it off. A loud silence assaults my ears. The sparks were so bright, the saw so loud, and now the cargo bay is awash with shadow. Yellow-white lights flicker in my vision, and I turn, heart pounding as if something might come lurching out of the edges of the room, the universe personified, reaching for me, pulling me away, away.

I blink and shake my head to clear it. But it has the opposite effect. The shadows begin to curdle and turn red, like thick crimson smoke. And the ringing, the humming in my ears intensifies. It coalesces and deepens, until it is a sonorous song, vibrating from outside of me, seeping into my bones, filling my ears and nose and mouth until I *am* the sound, a pulsating thing of muscle and blood and bone, fit to burst.

I lean over the worktable, elbows braced on its solidity, and I press my forehead to the surface, eyes squeezed shut. I take a long breath in, hold it, a long breath out. This is shock. This is trauma. This is my body revolting against the cognitive dissonance of this ship, this place.

Footsteps sound on the metal floor behind me. It's the night, coming to get me. It's the infinite dark, ready to swallow me up. It's the ghost of Vasilissa.

A hand presses my back, warm, between the shoulder blades. I jolt upward, a gasp dislodging itself from my lungs.

Onyx eyes meet mine. Dorian.

"You're panicking," he says, matter-of-fact. "Why?"

I glance over his shoulder, past him, into the shadowy edges of the cargo bay, expecting to see living forms there, or misshapen limbs reaching outward, extending toward me. But there's nothing. The shadows are only shadows.

He takes my head in his hands, forcing me to face him. This time, I can't look away. He feels so terribly human until our gazes meet. Until his eyes bore into me, showing me the most alien part of him, these twin pools of slick oil. His thumbs press to the muscle below my ears. His fingers dig into my hair at the base of my skull.

"Ami," he says, his voice a deep, low hum itself, as if he seeks to counteract the sound that haunts me. "Whatever you think you see, whatever has frightened you, it's not real. Do you understand?"

I nod.

"Do you *understand*?"

I pull my lips inward, biting at them, my chest on fire. Dorian holds me with his gaze, and I am a willing victim to it. Tilting my head into his hands, like a cat leaning into a delicate palm, I allow my eyes to flutter closed. Everywhere he touches me I'm alight, and my breaths are slowing, and I'm safe.

"Yes," I breathe at last. "I understand."

He leans forward. I feel his breath against my ear, and he presses a warm kiss to my temple. The movements are hesitant. Searching. Wondering. I'm a cornered animal, and any sudden action might send me into another panic. But the kiss, gentle as it is, chaste as it is, hits me like a storm. Every synapse in my brain lights up, and every muscle in my body relaxes, and all I feel is calm and safe and safe and *safe*. I've never been afraid in my life. How could I be? There's nothing in this universe that can hurt me.

"There," he says, pulling back slightly, but his lips brush my cheek as he speaks. "I have you. I'll keep you safe. There's nothing to be afraid of. Let go."

The ship's hum reverberates from within and without me, and this time, it is a balm. I drink it in like sweet syrupy wine, and it consumes me.

I wake up in my room, tucked in bed. I'm naked, except for my underwear. The lights are off, and for a moment I can see nothing but the illuminated viewscreen, the trail of lights across the blackness, stars and celestial bodies that shine eons away. My gaze darts to the far corner of the room, but there is nothing watching me, no glowing eyes, no Dorian-shaped silhouette clinging to the edges of my vision. I notice, then, that I'm not afraid. I didn't wake with a start, but with a satisfied sigh.

I'm safe. Dorian will keep me safe.

It occurs to me that I don't remember how I got here. I have no memory of leaving the cargo bay, returning to my room, or climbing into bed. The last thing I remember is Dorian, holding me against his chest, his lips to my skin.

And the ceaseless hum.

I should get out of bed and write this down. I should have records of every interaction, every strange occurrence. But I'm too tired, too relaxed. It doesn't matter. I'll do it when I wake. I'm perfectly safe.

I am back on *Pioneer*. Everything is brightly lit, sterile, and correct. When I glance out the airlock porthole, I see stars zipping past us like fireflies. I make my way down the ladder to the med bay, my footsteps muffled as I descend, my ears ringing.

Everything is white and bright and so spotless, and the longer I descend the ladder, the brighter it becomes, until my eyes sting.

At last, I drop down into the med bay, bypassing the last few rungs of the ladder, and there's hardly a sound as I hit the floor. I find it hard to walk; my feet lift slowly, impossibly heavy as if they're encased in concrete. But I have to get to the stasis pods. I can still save them. I can save Mahdi, his crooked smile. I can save Lily, her infectious laugh. I can save Vasilissa, who could have been a friend if we'd had more time.

I just have to get to them.

But the journey from the ladder across that tiny room is interminable. I'm wading through thick mud, my eyes streaming from the bright, blinding lights.

When at last I come to Vasilissa's pod, I'm breathing hard. So hard the sound fills up my ears until my skull is roaring with it.

I press the button to open her stasis pod, and the top slides back to free her, her gaunt face coming into view with terrible clarity. I go to Lily next, then Mahdi. One by one, their pods slide open.

I'm here to save you.

I stand there amongst them, the roar and ring of an endless sound in my head, squeezing my brain.

All I have to do is open you up.

I notice that I'm holding Vasilissa's comb. It's pinker than I remember, and the prongs are longer, sharper. They curve toward me, waving like tentacles.

Suddenly, with a sickening surge, Vasilissa sits up. Her body is rigid, her eyes wide, and she has no whites, no pupils or irises. Just black, black, horrible eyes that hold me. I can't move or speak or think. Blood-red swirls form in her gaze, like clouds of blood in dark waters, and she opens her mouth in a mirthless grin. Her lips split, and the skin of her face begins to slough off. Because she's dead. She's been dead for years. *Years.* And I opened the pod, and now she's decomposing, becoming a skeleton before my eyes, her skin and muscles falling off in horrible chunks, slithering down to the bed where she sits, staring at me, her eyes horrible and black, and red and shining.

"That's my comb," she says, reaching out for it. Her hand has lost its flesh, nothing now but a series of interlocking bones.

I'm shaking so hard I can barely hold the thing. I don't want it. "Take it," I manage, and I fling the comb toward her.

"Take it!" I scream as the plastic prongs lodge into one of her lidless eyes.

Take it!

I jolt awake, strangled cries frothing at the base of my throat, and I'm thrashing, blankets tangled about my legs. I lie half-sobbing in the dark, my breath a rasping choke. It was a dream. I close my eyes, hard, pressing my knuckles into the sockets. It was a dream. Opening my eyes again, I'm half-blinded by the shimmer of flashes in my vision. Sitting up, sweating and shaken, the light flares on and I blink, my gaze going immediately to the corners of the room.

Nothing is there.

"It was a dream," I insist, but I don't know who I'm trying to convince.

11

THERE IS a new corridor outside my room. It has appeared, seemingly, out of nowhere, branching off a few steps past my door. There are now two corridors: the one I've been up and down and never able to walk beyond twelve paces; and this new one, perpendicular to the original, and trailing off into what appears to be an interminable distance. Not far down it, the lights are off, and the passage is swallowed up in darkness.

I need to go that way. I know this immediately. Somehow, for some reason, the ship has chosen to let me see this new hallway. Or the ship has slipped up, arranging itself in an unplanned way, and I've stumbled upon a mistake. But both options mean one thing: this corridor is important. There's no time to make up my mind. I've only just left my room, still sleep-addled and chilled with half-dried sweat. My feet make the decision before I do.

I walk down the new corridor. It feels just like the other one, but the ship's distant hum permeates my thoughts as I move slowly down the hallway. Lights begin to flicker on as

I go, thank God. I don't want to walk in darkness, but I know that I would have.

There's something in this corridor that's waiting for me.

This hallway doesn't loop. After thirteen steps, I glance over my shoulder and see the way I've come. I take a few more steps, and I am still here, proceeding down the new corridor. I am not being led in a circle.

An eager fear boils at the base of my chest, and I am wide-eyed and breathing heavily, waiting — expecting — *wanting* — something to stop me in my tracks. I realize that the hum is getting even louder. It's a buzz, a cry, and a breath; waves lapping at the curve of my skull. I hate it. And when it begins to hurt, when I've been walking for what feels like hours, I stop. I want to turn back, but I can't.

Why am I wandering down this endless corridor, and what do I hope I'll find?

Thrum, thrum, thrum.

I stumble, the sound in my head so loud now that it's vice-like on my psyche, and my jaw aches from it, and my eye sockets threaten to expel my eyeballs from the pressure. I take another step forward, obstinate. I refuse to let fear rule me, to stop me from finding whatever waits for me at the end of this...

My knee buckles slightly. I don't know if it's the sound in my ears or my fear taking hold. Putting out a hand to steady myself, I lean my weight against the wall, breathing hard.

"You're fine," I murmur. "You're fine. You're tired and traumatized. You're exploring. Just exploring. There's nothing waiting for you."

The words offer a small amount of comfort. I know all

about verbal output; how saying a thing out loud makes your brain more liable to believe it. The thought strengthens me just a little, slowing the gallop of my frightened heart. I *want* to explore. I want to see what's down this corridor.

Every terror I've experienced, every movement in the shadows, it hasn't been real. It's all been a dream, in my head. There's no danger.

When I finally catch my breath, I push off from the wall and... there's something sticky on my hand.

I look down.

The palm of my hand is red. Not red from cold or heat. No, it's drenched in liquid, *deep* red, thick, and sticky, and it drips down my wrist. It smells metallic and vivid.

It's blood.

Breath catches in my throat, and I spin to face the wall where I'd been resting my hand. There is no blood. It's just textured metal, clean, absolutely clean.

"...the *hell*," I breathe.

I hold up my palm, and the blood is still there. Disgusted and confused, I wipe it feverishly against the leg of my jumpsuit. Get it off. Get it *off*! But the liquid won't budge, my hand is stained with it. It's dripping down my wrist and arm, pooling at my elbow, this horrible thick red fluid.

"What the *fuck*." My voice cracks.

Still rubbing my palm on my jumpsuit, I spin around, glancing wildly behind me, into the distant shadows, the claws of fear tightening at my throat. And then I stop. I freeze in place, heart hammering in my ears.

Because the ship's hum is an overwhelming storm.

Because there is blood on my hand. Because I don't remember which direction I came from.

In my panic, I turned myself around. Both directions look identical now, an empty corridor disappearing into shadow.

I'm lost.

The thought repeats itself in my head like a marquee, in great flashing neon. *Lost, lost, lost.* Covered in blood.

I let out a strangled scream and rush forward, not caring whether I'm heading back to my room or hurtling deeper into the ship. I just want to get away from the blood wall. If I run far enough, my hand will be clean. The hum in my ears will go away. I will become clean.

I don't know how long I run, my lungs are on fire, and I'm terrified to look at my dripping red hand, the bleeding ship. The hallway is endless, never changing, lights flickering on as I move forward, blackness behind and before me.

And then, when I'm sure I'm about to pass out from exertion and terror, I see it: a door.

It can't be my room. I would have noticed the branching corridor; I've been stumbling straight forward. Haven't I? The door stares at me with its unassuming visage, plain metal. Daring me.

Would opening the door be better than racing down this endless hallway?

I only pause long enough to catch my breath for a moment, and then I open the door, practically falling over the threshold. An orange light flickers on, and the door clicks shut behind me.

I'm breathing hard. Tears of fear and exhaustion prick

at my eyes. This is my room. There is the bed, and the table, and everything else... except that none of my things are here. There is no pothos here. It's completely empty.

Lifting my hands, I gaze at the palms, a feeling of slow suffocation lodges at the base of my throat, just above my collarbones. I'm clean. There's no blood. No thick, choking red. I turn my hand around, then bend down to look at my jumpsuit. There's no trace of it, that horrible... horrible redness, soaking me.

Swallowing the pit in my throat, I sit on the bed before my knees give way. Did I imagine it? No; it was so real. It wasn't a dream. This is *not* a dream. I woke up already.

All the while, the distant sound pushes against my brain. A buzzy echo in my skull.

I decide that I imagined the blood on my hand. Hallucinated it. Who wouldn't, in deep space?

"I'm operating under extreme conditions," I say aloud, my voice quiet and wobbling. "Humans are not meant to spend years in stasis, or meet aliens, or encounter spaceships that don't look the way they actually look." I take a deep, slow breath. Of course. Of *course*. "It's the ship." My voice grows steadier, and the sound of my own confidence helps calm my nerves. The distant hum seems almost friendly now, a warmth in my core.

"The ship's frequency is confusing my brain," I continue. "Maybe it's a glitch, a bug. I thought I saw blood that wasn't there. But it wasn't real." I'm almost delirious now, searching for an explanation that makes sense. "It wasn't real. I wasn't hallucinating, not really. I'm not going mad. It's always the ship."

A wave of relief washes over me. It's all fine. I'll just

stay here for a moment, collect myself, and then call for Dorian. He'll help me find my way back to my room.

Sighing, I flop backwards on the bed. I might even take a nap, or — I freeze. Something's digging into my back. Irritated, I sit up, reaching under the blanket to remove the offending object. I hold it up.

A pencil.

I peer at the wooden thing, momentarily confused, almost dumbstruck. What is a pencil doing here? Then I begin to see it, really see it, and all at once I'm sick to my stomach. I know this pencil. It's pockmarked with indentations, dozens of little bite marks where someone dug their teeth into the wood. On one side of the pencil are the faded blue letters M.M.

I *know* this pencil.

This is Mahdi's pencil. I've seen him hold it between his teeth like a Spanish dancer holds a rose. Watched him tap it against his temple, his knuckles. He fidgets — *used* to fidget with it, constantly. It was his.

All my hard-won calm immediately dissolves.

I'm encased in ice, unable and unwilling to fully grasp what I'm holding. Could it be another glitch? But why? Why this, why these specific objects?

Shaking so hard I can hardly manage it, I reach into my jumpsuit pocket and take out Vasilissa's comb. I hold the two items side by side. They should not be on this ship. They *are not* on this ship.

Aren't they?

"Dorian," I say, the name catching in my throat, faint and frightened. "Dorian."

He's my anchor, why shouldn't I call for him? He's

done nothing but soothe me. Everything is too loud, and too quiet, and he's all I have, just now.

Slowly, I get up from the bed, overcome with the horrible and overwhelming sense that Mahdi has been here. In this very room. He's been here, slept here, chewed that pencil here.

But he couldn't have been. Mahdi is dead.

My chin shakes and my fingers shake and everything is shaking and I'm cold and I'm lost in this ship and the distant thrum is inside of me, everywhere, caressing me, nuzzling at my organs, and Mahdi was in this room.

A scream or a sob begins to work its way up my throat. I don't want to let it out; I'm afraid that if I do, something will hear me and silence me with gentle hands, and I'll be lost forever.

The door clicks open.

12

"AMI." My name in his mouth: a question and a consolation.

I'm in his arms before I have a chance to stop myself. He is my only comfort here, the only warm thing, the only embrace. And in my terror, as the hum invades my senses, I'm desperate for him. He takes me in as if he was born to hold me, enveloping me with arms around my body and a cheek on the top of my head, my chest against his, our heartbeats hammering in tandem.

"Shh," he says as I gasp and sob, his fingers drawing slow strokes down my hair, thumbing the base of my skull. "Don't worry. You're safe. I will not let anything harm you. You're safe."

I believe him.

My hands clutch at the back of his shirt, as if I'm going to fall the moment I let him go and wake up frozen in a stasis pod, trapped between life and death. If I let him go, I'll run forever down a bleeding corridor. Or I'll fall down a depthless well, the ship's hum surrounding me until I fracture into a billion particles.

"I was afraid this would happen," he breathes, almost inaudible. As if he's talking to himself, far away. "I tried to warn you... I can't control it..."

None of his words make sense to me. They don't have to. I lift my head to face him, this being who is not human but who feels, smells, sounds so deeply familiar that my chest aches. My vision swims with tears, my face wet, my nose clogged.

When I reach up to tangle my fingers in his hair, pulling his face down to mine, there is no thought involved. I don't plan it. I simply open my mouth to his and drink him in.

He responds the way a human would. His shoulders relax and he melts into me, both tightening his grip and softening. A low sound in his throat says he's enjoying this. His fervent return of the kiss says he's been wanting this.

I begin to drown in the feel of him. I'm overflowing, clutching at him for dear life, and all around me the walls are crowding in, red and slick, and the *thrum, thrum, thrum* drones at the base of my fragile skull.

We stumble to the bed like a pair of horny teenagers. I am drunk on him, and I need him to keep me intoxicated, keep his warm mouth on mine, his hands seeking, my nerves alight. I'm already forgetting what had frightened me. It doesn't matter, now that Dorian's here. He presses a thumb to the base of my throat and kisses me slowly, his body weighing me down. I couldn't escape if I wanted to.

And I *don't* want to. I want to be here, yes, right here, and nowhere else, forever.

"Ami," he groans. "I've waited so long for you."

I don't know what that means, and I don't care. Maybe I've waited for him too. I came all this way, light-years and light-years, and I found him. Why shouldn't I surrender to this?

He unzips my jumpsuit, warming me with kisses beneath my ear and down my neck, to the soft curves of my breasts. My back arches and I can't have enough; I need more, more, *more*. I am open to him, ready and eager. I'm open to the encroaching darkness and its reaching tendrils, to the ship closing in and in around us, umbral and unending.

13

STARS GLITTER, dreamlike, through the massive window of the docking bay. I'm standing just inside the forcefield that prevents me from being swept out to space, and I can feel its powerful electric murmur like a million insects.

The stars are radiant. There are so many of them, an impossible array, and utterly unfamiliar. I feel like a teenager again, lying on a cramped stretch of rooftop with my boyfriend, a thin blanket draped across the corrugated metal that digs into our backs, gazing up at a meteor shower. The main thing I remember about that night is the cold. We were crowded together for warmth, even in our coats and hats on that unusually clear, November night. And every time a falling piece of space debris made its fiery way through the Earth's atmosphere, we gasped and cheered. Sometimes there were three or four at once, cutting golden arcs over us. Eventually, we grew too cold to watch the display, and focused our attention instead on staying warm, and on each other.

But he ended up hurting me, just like all the others.

I falter where I stand, blinking hard. A flash of a memory assaults my senses: Dorian's body, his hands caressing a symphony on my skin, sweat and heaving breaths and moans of pleasure.

My cheeks heat, my skin tingles. I thought — no, I'm here. In the docking bay. Only, I can't remember how I got here. The last thing I remember is Dorian. And...

I shove my hands in my pockets and feel the objects waiting there: the comb, the chewed pencil.

There's a sound behind me. The quiet, deliberate shuffle of footsteps that don't wish to be heard. I turn, heart pounding.

No one's there.

Only *Pioneer*, a dark shape in the gloomy bay; and beyond her, the comms array.

But it's gone. The comms array, the one I was nearly done repairing, is gone. So is my work table, and the collection of tools. I move haltingly toward where the table had been, wanting to confirm what I'm seeing, but my feet are like lead.

"Mahdi?" I say, senselessly.

I finger the comb in my pocket.

"Vasilissa?" The name is painful in my dry throat. I'm calling out for ghosts. No one will respond; I know that. I do.

"They're dead," I announce, but my words come out like choked-up splinters. "I finished fixing the array, and Dorian moved it somewhere. Maybe it's attached to the ship again." But my own words don't convince me. I walk around *Pioneer* until I see where the comms array should be. It's not there. Nor is it anywhere in the docking bay. It's not a small contraption, not easily hidden. There's nothing here but me and *Pioneer* and a few large boxes in the corner.

"What did you do with it?" I breathe, and I don't know who I'm asking.

There's no answer. Only the deep breathing of Dorian's ship, the thrumming in my skull and in my veins.

A movement catches my eye. A shadow, darting behind *Pioneer*.

My pulse races, my scalp prickling. There was something familiar about that shadow. Something strangely intimate, a shape I know well, and she's calling to me. *Lily*.

"Wait," I say, rushing forward. "Lily!"

But when I come around the other side of *Pioneer*, no one's there. I would have heard footsteps if she was running from me. If anyone was here, I would have heard them.

She's not here.

She's haunting me, I think wildly. They all are. It's unfair that I'm alive and they're not, that I survived stasis. It's unfair that their bodies are frozen, preserved in dreamless sleep, while I...

"It's not my fault," I snap, as if Lily is standing before me, arms folded, one eyebrow raised in chastisement. "I couldn't have done anything."

But a sickly guilt froths in my stomach like acid, an accusation. I'm here, and they're not.

"I couldn't have done anything," I say again, weakly this time, backing away from this imaginary Lily. "I was asleep too."

And then Lily is *there*.

Solid, colorful, human. But her eyes are wide and unearthly, and as she moves toward me, her face begins to contort. A dark stain appears on her chest, spreading, dark dark red, blood seeping from a wound.

I take a step back, but Lily moves closer still, closing the gap between us, and I smell the burning scent of iron and fear and terror.

"Look," says Lily, wrenching open her shirt. She is naked beneath, and between her breasts gapes a deep, angry wound. So deep, I see her heart beating through it, jagged edges of her ribs peeking whitely out through gore.

I can't look away. My own heart threatens to judder and stop. My feet are frozen to the spot.

"*Look!*" she insists again, and the wound grows larger, spilling red-black blood down her front.

I'm looking, I try to object, to make her understand. I *am* looking, I see you, I'm sorry. I'm sorry. There was nothing I could do. I was asleep. *I was asleep*.

But no words come; my throat is closed, my heartbeat erratic. I think I might pass out from fear. My fingers close around Mahdi's pencil, and I try to scream, but nothing comes out.

As if to mock me, Lily opens her mouth wide, grinning in hideous silence.

And then, just as suddenly as she appeared, Lily is gone.

Shaking uncontrollably, I fall to my knees. I can't catch my breath. The docking bay walls close in, close in, and the ship's thrum grows louder in every cell of my body, as if its droning echo might soothe me.

It's only when I try to wipe the tears from my face that

I notice my hand. The palm is pierced where I clutched at Mahdi's pencil in my pocket, where its sharpened tip drove into my flesh. But I feel nothing. There's a smear of blood across my palm, and the pencil, when I inspect it, is stained red.

"I need a bandage," I murmur. I struggle slowly to my feet.

Returning the pencil to my pocket, I leave the docking bay. And with every step, I feel that I am being watched.

———

"Dorian?" I need him.

I've only gone a few paces, just beyond the docking bay, when I hear his footsteps. He comes up behind me, and I turn to face him. By now, I'm used to this, or maybe even numb to it: his appearances in my blind spots, as if I won't notice that he's appearing from nowhere. But even with this knowledge, it's like the fear I should be feeling, the dread at his spectral approach, won't surface. Instead, I feel my terror and dread subsiding into a distant murmur of comforting sound.

He won't hurt me. He has promised it again and again: I'm safe.

The moment he catches my gaze, his expression seems to crumple, and he rushes to me. "Ami," he says, crowding into me, cupping my face in his hands. His black hair falls around our faces like a curtain as he kisses me just above one eye, his lower lip brushing my eyelid. "You're frightened. Tell me what happened."

I lean into his touch. And as I do, the ship's hum overwhelms me, deeply vibrating in my gut, my brain. "I thought..." I begin, unsure what to say. Where do I start?

"You can tell me," he murmurs, warm lips against my ear, his hand at the nape of my neck, holding me close. "You saw something. Tell me."

I fight back tears. "My crew," I manage. "I keep seeing them. Imagining them. Only, it feels real. They're angry with me. And... when you and I... when you came to me, in that room that wasn't mine..." I try to pull away just enough to look up at him, to meet his gaze, but he holds me tight against him, enveloped in his body heat.

"Do you regret it?" he asks, his voice soft.

Something in me rebels at the question. I can't stand that he asked it, that he'd doubt me. The sharp tang of conflicting emotions try to rise to the surface. But his warm touch, his slowly rising and falling chest, soothe me, and the feeling fades.

"No," I answer at last. "Of course I don't." It isn't a lie. "But I was lost in a new corridor, and when I touched the walls, my hand... it came away bloody. And then you came to me, and I..." I trail off, not knowing what else to say, or how to articulate my confusion.

And then I was here. I don't *remember*. How did I get here?

"You've been deeply traumatized," he says, voice sweet in my ear. "No other human has ever experienced what you've been through. What you're *going* through. You're light-years from home. Grieving. My ship is not accustomed to your brain chemistry, and it's likely having a negative effect on your mental state. I thought it couldn't possibly harm you, that all you'd experience was alteration of the senses..."

He trails off, but his fingers remain in my hair, stroking, and I am melting into it. Everything he says rings true. I *am* traumatized. Grieving. Experiencing things the human mind was never meant to endure.

But something in me flickers, a distant incredulity. "Dorian, are you saying that the bleeding walls, my dead crew, they're hallucinations?"

"Yes," he purrs. "Nothing will hurt you. None of it is real."

My gut tightens in a sick knot. I move away from him, and the effort it takes to leave his embrace is almost overwhelming. He watches me almost warily, heavy-lidded, brows drawn low. I reach into my pockets, one by one, and take out the comb. The pencil. "Are *these* a hallucination?"

For one mad, fraction of a second, I think he's going to attack me. His gaze darkens, his nostrils flare, and a shadow passes over his unearthly features, rendering him terrifying and inescapable, an apex predator ready to spring.

But as soon as the expression twists his features, it's gone again. And he is soft once more, empathetic, comforting.

"I told you," he says, taking a step toward me, closing the distance I created between us. "My ship is adjusting to your physiology, the complex synapses in your brain. Some of the things you're seeing, touching, hearing — they aren't real. Not in the way you think they are. It's the ship's way of protecting your mind."

"This is Vasilissa's comb," I insist shrilly, holding it up, its pink plastic catching the light. "And Mahdi's pencil. I know these objects. They're *here now*. Solid. Not hallucinations. Isn't that what you said about the food? The pothos? Is any of this real or not?"

Dorian's mouth curves in sympathy. "Ami, deep space was always going to have this effect on the human mind. The experiments your space travel organizations conducted, even within the Sol System—"

"Look!" I insist, panicked anger roiling in my chest. I hold up my hand, palm outward. The skin is still marred, still sticky with drying blood where Mahdi's pencil pierced the skin. "Is this a hallucination?"

His gaze remains locked on my face. "I don't know what you want me to say."

I open my mouth to demand an explanation, some measure of clarity, but the words won't come. How am I meant to argue against him, against a being who sees something utterly different than what I do? We're two living things, both made of flesh and blood, but our realities are light-years apart. What does this ship look like to him? Am I even holding a comb and a pencil, or are my hands empty? Nausea rises in my belly at the thought.

He doesn't even hear the thrum.

"The comms array," I gasp, almost pleading, a last-ditch attempt to make him understand my fear.

He raises an eyebrow.

"It's gone. Not in the docking bay, not reinstalled on my ship. It's *gone*."

"I didn't move it, if that's what you're implying."

I almost sob with frustration. "I'm not implying anything. I'm confused. Things don't make sense here. Things appear and disappear. I wander in circles. There was *blood* on my hand, and I'm being haunted, or—" My voice breaks. "I don't know what to do."

"Don't worry," he says, pulling me to him. And I let him, the fight leaving me as quickly as it came. He kisses my forehead, runs his fingers through my hair. The deep and fervent hum, ever present, wraps me in its sound and soothes the rough edges of my thoughts. I relax into him. I breathe deeply, inhaling him, and slowly, the fractures in my world begin to heal.

"You're safe," he says, a chant, a prayer. "Let go. You found me. I have you."

There's a muffled clatter as something hits the metal floor — the comb, the pencil.

"I have you," Dorian murmurs again, and his words entwine with the distant hum, curling into my ear and filling me up. "You're safe. Stay. Stay with me."

I have no choice in the matter. The ship's hum serenades me, and Dorian is everything, strong hands and safety and the ship itself, wrapping me up warm and tight, tight, tight. Holding me and never letting go.

14

HE MAKES love to me in the corridor.

I kiss him, hungry, and he knows exactly where and how to touch me; how to make my body and mind completely helpless. He's painfully real to me, and I need him, and his low murmurs of satisfaction wind through me like a thread of comfort.

I fumble at the fastening of his antiquated trousers, yanking his starched collar open, my teeth at his collarbone, a desperate and frenzied undressing.

He fills me up, rolling into and against me, hot and vivid. There's an ache deep inside me and it grows with each of his thrusts until I'm gasping, crying out his name. He is everywhere and everything. He holds my thighs apart with strong hands, groaning in my ear, calling me by name: *Ami, Ami, stay with me. Stay.* He comes with a low groan. I tighten around him, wracked by my drawn-out pleasure, until I feel that I'm no longer here. No longer human or corporeal.

I've ascended, or crumbled to dust, and his heaving form contains the universe of me.

And then Dorian is no longer Dorian. He is smaller, softer.

I pull away, still overflowing with desire, and I'm wrapped in Lily's arms. She's naked, her eyes hazy with lust, her lips pink and swollen. She tilts her head, breathing hard, her long lashes glowing red, red in the corridor's light.

"Ami," she croons, running a finger down my throat, "Don't you want me? I thought we had something."

I freeze. I want to push her away. I'm desperate to close my eyes, to erase the burning image of my dead lover. But I can't. I'm captive to her. I try to speak, but my words dry up, shriveling like rotted flesh.

Lily makes an exaggerated face, pouting. "I asked you a question, Ami. What did I do wrong? I thought you cared about me."

"No," I manage, a pathetic, weak, rattle of a word. I try to escape, but I am helpless, my muscles atrophied in fear.

The ship's hum grows louder, pulsating, an enormous heartbeat, until I'm deafened.

"No, what?" Lily demands, her voice cutting through the noise like heated steel. Her eyes are wild, and her face begins to morph, to become something monstrous, unrecognizable. Her voice echoes through me, painful with every reverberation. "You can't deny it," she spits. "We all saw what you did. I'll show you."

And she begins to unfold her skin, peeling it away as if it's a garment, revealing bright red blood and sinew and moon-white bone, pulsing veins, glistening muscle.

I scream, at last, and everything goes dark.

I am alone in my room.

It feels like I blinked, and suddenly, Lily was gone. And now I'm here. My jumpsuit is zipped up to the throat, covering my trembling body, though I still feel horribly exposed. The ship's insidious hum drowns out my thudding heart.

I stumble, rubbing a hand across my face.

A moment ago, Lily was showing me her insides. Before that, my back was pressed to the wall, my thighs still sweat-slick around Dorian's hips. But here I stand, as if... as if it was a dream. Like neither of them were ever here. But my skin is hot and tender, my lips still swollen. Hardly daring to breathe, I unzip my jumpsuit, slowly, just enough to reach my hand inside, down between my legs.

I'm wet, my underwear soaked through. And when I pull my hand away, holding it up to the light, there is thick white cum on my fingers.

"No," I whisper. How long have I been standing here? How long have I been alone in my room, fucked and left to forget?

Why can't I remember?

"Dorian." My voice is weak, fractured. I refuse to think of Lily. I refuse to accept the grotesque vision of her. And as soon as I make this refusal, the memory begins to fade. I imagined her in a fit of emotion. I made her up in my fear and pleasure, mixing and muddling my emotions.

"Dorian," I say again. There's panic in my voice. My body detaches from me, as if my heartbeat is drifting slowly away into the night, my shaking fingers fading from view, and I'm but a solitary speck in the stretch of endless stars.

Thoughtlessly, I push my hands into my pockets, searching for comfort or perhaps a reminder. But my pockets are empty. I feel distinctly that I put something there, that I was saving it. But it's gone now. Did I drop something?

I look to the floor, and my heart skips.

There are red, liquid footsteps there: My footsteps. They lead from the door to where I'm standing, only a few paces, yet they're clear as day: Blood. Thick and wet. Just like the blood I had seen on my hands.

Fear comes racing back, and I embrace it, clutching it with desperate fingers. It's all that reminds me of who I am, *what* I am. I'm human. On a mission. In an alien ship.

I know that I should inspect the footprints. Maybe it's a trick of the light. Another vision, a hallucination. But my pulse screams danger, my lungs constrict, and I'm choked by the need to get away. Far, far away. Off this ship. If I run fast and far enough, I'll leave the bloody footprints behind, and they will fade into nothing but memory, and one day, that memory will disappear altogether.

I burst from my room and run pell-mell through the ship's corridors. I pass another door to my room, then another just like it, and another. Or maybe they're not my room; maybe the ship has finally opened up to me, allowing me to wander it fully, unsupervised. Or perhaps I'm simply dashing in a terrified circle, eating my own tail like a doomed ouroboros.

My lungs burn. I begin to stumble, weakening,

succumbing to the heavy weight of dread and the limits of my already low stamina.

A new corridor suddenly opens to my left, and I pelt down it. My vision blurs with tears, or fear, or both. My lungs scream for air, but I don't stop running. I have to keep going. I have to get *away*.

The light is dimmer now, or maybe it's the walls that are darkening, crimson, rich, and sanguine, dripping like wet paint.

These corridors run thick with blood. Have they always?

My boots slide on gore. It's like the floors have been flayed open, revealing living tissue beneath, and the thrum is the ship itself breathing, the sound of life coursing through this thing that has eaten me, swallowed me whole, and there is nowhere to go but deeper inside.

And as I go it gets louder, *louder*, a percussive pulse against my eardrums, my brain, my entire body. If it doesn't exist but I hear it, and I feel it, doesn't that make it real?

Things begin to move on the walls as I pass. I don't want to see; I refuse to look at whatever is slowly emerging, undulating in shadow.

I won't look.

But I have to.

My footsteps slow, my lungs fight for breath, and my muscles scream from overuse. I pause for a breath, for two, three. The walls swim like black-red soup, and something crawls, or swims, or drags itself up alongside me.

A body, drenched in blood. Naked. Shriveled like a revenant.

It reaches for me, its eyes wide.

I trip over my feet and fall backward, catching myself painfully with my elbows on the floor. I try to scramble away from the thing, but my boots can't find purchase in the gory muck.

"Ami," the thing says, a keening, pleading sound.

It's Mahdi's voice.

There's not enough breath in my lungs, not enough strength in me to reply. To tell it that it doesn't exist, to leave me the fuck alone. It is *not real*.

But even as I force myself to my feet, the red-orange light refracting off my tears and confusing my vision, I don't believe my own fervent thoughts. It *is* real. Mahdi is as real as the horror in my heart, as the blood staining my jumpsuit.

I can't stay here in this corridor of blood. I know that I have to get away. And I'm still certain that if I run far enough, I'll find a way out. I don't know if I'm racing toward the docking bay or deeper inside the ship, but I can't stay where I am. Because the body is behind me, slithering through the thick tissue of the walls. And then another *thing* joins it in my blurry periphery. Another body? A figment? They follow me as I run, as I move through the vessel toward the heart of every terror that has woken me in the night and left me gagging on dread.

"Ami." It's Lily's voice.

"Ami, wait," says Vasilissa.

They are all here with me, my crew. These horrible ghoulish bodies, dragging themselves along the walls, the ceiling above me. I sob, a sharp and painful act, my lungs on the verge of giving out. What if I let them have me? Me, who survived when they didn't? What if I let them exact whatever revenge they think I deserve?

Thrum, thrum, thrum.

My bones vibrate with the sound. It's embedded in me now. A parasite, unseen, clinging to my nerves. Holding my heart in a web of forceful thread.

AMI. WHERE DO YOU THINK YOU'LL GO NOW?

I skid to a sudden halt. Before me lies a sanguine wall. There's nowhere to go from here but back the way I came. And behind me, I hear the slithering, juddering movements of my crew, their muffled murmurs, their cajoling.

But wait — there's a door. It's black, devoid of light, as if the night has carved itself a space in the wall.

GO INSIDE. FIND WHAT YOU'VE BEEN LOOKING FOR.

"Why did you leave us?" Lily's voice is thick behind me, and I spin to face her, this human-shaped thing rising up from the ichor-thick floor. Sticky tendrils coat her hair and body, filaments of living matter, as if she's being born from the corridor itself.

"I didn't," I croak, backing away. "You died in stasis."

Lily's face is as I remember it on *Pioneer*, gaunt, deathly pale, but blood-spattered and draped with gory webbing, clots of dark crimson clinging to her forehead, her cheeks. She reaches for me, and I stumble backward.

"Ami," she says. Thick bubbles of blood ooze from the corner of her mouth. "I trusted you. I loved you. But the others saw what I didn't. They left bits of themselves for you to find. They knew you better than me."

"I didn't do *anything*," I protest, shrill, and as I move away from Lily, my back hits something solid. The black door. I'm shaking, stricken, terror clotting in my throat. She's going to kill me. She's going to wrap her gore-wet hands around my throat and drag me down, down into the corridor's bloody tissue until we're all submerged, drowned, digested by the ship.

Lily's eyes flash with madness. "You did this to me." Her voice is a roiling, painful hatred. "*You did this to me.*"

She lunges, just as I reach behind me and push on the door. It falls open, and I am falling too, into the blackness beyond.

15

THE DOOR SLAMS BEHIND ME, abruptly cutting off Lily's voice. I'm plunged into silence. I've been swallowed whole, just as I feared. Thick air fills my lungs, like each breath is a drink of fetid water. I'm on my hands and knees on a floor that's uneven, soft, and gummy. Everything is warm and wet.

Slowly, I stand.

I was wrong — this place is not silent. I'm in the sonorous dark, wrapped tightly in the bosom of the *thrum, thrum, thrum*. It's so loud, so unceasing and all-consuming that I am part of it now.

The room swims into focus around me. My eyes are adjusting, and the ambient red-orange light brightens as I stagger, disoriented. I blink through my tears, brushing them away.

My breath catches.

I'm not in a room — it's a cavern. A vast reach of pulsing red. As the shadows fade, I try to make sense of where I am. It's unlike anything I've ever seen.

The enormous space, this humid expanse, is dark and mottled red. From the floor to the ceiling, it glistens like the inside of an organ. As if I've fallen into a massive stomach or aorta. The walls pulsate, moving slowly in and out, like the breaths of a living thing. And protruding outward from the ceiling, floor, and walls, are throbbing, slick, ichorous growths. Like tumors the size of houses. Countless thick filaments of vibrating tissue converge on each of these masses, connecting them from the ceiling to the floor and the walls, a latticed network of living matter.

Thrum, thrum, thrum roars inside every cell of me.

And I realize: this room, these pulsing organs, *they* are causing the sound. Is it the flow of blood? A biological engine? A song with no melody? A drawn-out cry of pain?

If this is a language, it's like nothing I've ever heard before. It's beyond my understanding. All I can think is that I *have* been swallowed. I am inside something alive.

But these thoughts are hardly realized; they ricochet in my mind and then fade, like skipping stones sinking into deep waters. The sound gathers my thoughts in a steel-tight grip, crushing them. It burrows into me, my bones, my soul. My head throbs in pain. It's not just the sound — there's a tension in here, as if the humid air is electrified, as if with every inhale, I'm drawing something foreign into me. Letting it consume and change me.

Ami.

My name rings so loud and heavy in my head that I nearly lose my balance and fall again. I glance down, shaking, and see that my hands are red and wet. *Is it blood? Or is it something else?*

Hot, thick liquid drips down my upper lip. I press the

back of one knuckle to the skin, and it comes away bright crimson. My nose is bleeding.

DON'T FIGHT IT.

The voice, the *thought*, the sound... it pierces my consciousness with excruciating precision. I've never felt pain like it, as if my soul is being autopsied, as if my thoughts are held victim to a white-hot blade and observed with cool finality.

"Stop," I sob, covering my ears with helpless hands.

DON'T FIGHT IT. LET ME IN.

I choke on another sob, and my knees give way at last. And finally, I understand. It, they, whatever this place is... it's communicating with me. These words reverberate through the endless hum.

"Stop," I beg, my voice strangled with pain. I want to explain that it hurts, that this voice is a thousand daggers to my brain, that I'm *losing* my mind. That I've already lost it. But I'm doubled over in agony, my nose gushing blood, every muscle in my body taut with panic.

Please stop, I try to say again.

But it is never-ending.

I pull my hands from my face, seeking air, unable to breathe, and my palms are soaked in blood. More blood, thicker, brighter. Mine. Choking, I rub the back of my sleeve against my eyes to clear them. It stings and I gasp, dark spots marring my vision. My sleeve comes away red.

I'm weeping blood.

Whatever this room is, it's going to kill me. I'm too weak to withstand its voice. My human brain is too small, too delicate, not enough. And worst of all, some exhausted part of me wants to let the vibrating sound, and this room, consume me. I want to be swept up, cracked open, absorbed into all this pulsing, living matter.

I feel hands under my armpits, pulling me to my feet. I'm pressed to a firm chest as arms wrap around me. A low voice caresses me, murmuring words I don't understand.

The painful overwhelm begins to fade.

It's lessening like a receding tide, dulling to a distant hum. The pain, too, retreats, and my body relaxes, threatening to crumple.

But he holds me steady.

"Ami."

I don't have the strength to open my eyes, to look up at him, but I know it's Dorian.

"You shouldn't be in here," he says. "You could have lost your mind."

I retch, expelling something thick and phlegm-like onto his shirt. I don't care if he minds. I refuse to open my eyes. I refuse to see if what I've coughed up is more of my blood.

"Dorian," I manage, voice pale and broken. I feel half-dead. The room is spinning, even with my eyes closed, and the thrum, quieter though it is, remains inside me. "What *is* this?"

His thumb rubs circles into my hip, his other hand holding my head against his chest. "I didn't mean for you to come here. My ship should not have allowed it."

"A voice was talking to me," I say wetly, and spit more blood. My stomach lurches, and for a moment I'm afraid I'll truly vomit. "That sound... the sound you can't hear. It's a *voice*."

Dorian's quiet for a moment, though his caresses never cease. Then he presses a kiss to the top of my head. "I'm sorry," he says. "We underestimated the effects we would have on the human brain. When you came in here, we... Well, this is the first time we've truly seen you. If we had known, I wouldn't have allowed you to..."

He trails off, none of his words making sense.

At last, I dredge up the strength to open my eyes, and I pull away from him. He watches me with wide, sorrowful eyes, his hands outstretched as if waiting for me to come back to his embrace.

"What is this room?" I demand, my voice hoarse, barely above a whisper. "What is this ship? What is—" My stomach lurches as I realize, belatedly, what he said. *The effects we'd have. The first time we've truly seen you.* "Dorian. Who's *we*?"

His face falls. It's a surrender, as if he's been dreading this moment. In the red-orange light, his pale face is sickly, his black hair shining like hellfire. His eyes, though, won't let me go. His gaze holds me like a pearl in the palm.

"I'll explain, but not here. Come."

"No." I'm resolute, though every cell in my body rejects this place, screams at me to obey him. "Tell me now."

"This room is the energy source of my ship. The core of its functions. Maybe even what you'd call its beating heart, its brain. It is alive. Just like the ship is alive." He pauses, hesitating. "And I..."

I'm hardly breathing as he speaks. Something begins to fall into place. An organic ship, a beating heart, an endless humming sound pressing against my thoughts. A man who appears out of nowhere, who looks human and is anything but.

"And you?" I murmur, knowing the answer already.

He smiles, almost sadly. "I *am* the ship."

The knife of this truth lodges in my ribs. We stare at one another, the crimson room pulsing all around us.

"Ami," he says, placating. He reaches out a hand.

I take a step back. "The *ship*."

"Yes."

I swallow, tasting iron. "How?"

"I don't know how to explain it to you in a way you'd understand. Not fully, or accurately. But..." he tilts his head. "Your human concept of a hive mind. Of a colony of bees, or perhaps a school of fish. Each organism works in tandem, communicating seamlessly, acting as one for a singular goal. I am like that. We are like that. This ship contains many, but we are essentially one. One consciousness, one being. I'm simply the voice. The representative."

"No, that's insane," I blurt, as if my refusal will change the truth. But I know, even as I back away from him, that he's not lying. I can feel it in the ship's hum. I can feel *him* in it. He's here, in this room, all around me, inside me.

"I won't hurt you," Dorian says, but the promise has lost all meaning. "I never—"

"You never what?" I spit, enraged. "Never meant to hurt me? But you did. Look at me. I'm bleeding from the inside out. I'm losing blocks of time. My dead crew follows me, haunts me... I'm seeing things that can't be real. Unless they... *are* they real? How should I know what's possible in this fucking place?" I glance over my shoulder, relieved to see the door still behind me.

"Ami..."

"*Stop*," I almost shriek, my voice broken and terror-hoarse. "For all I know, this is some kind of game to you. An experiment to see how long the lost human survives inside your ship's *brain* before she loses her mind."

"Please," Dorian says. "I didn't realize how badly your psyche would be affected. That the ship's mind would consume you, coerce you, make you see such painful images. I didn't mean to. I have no control over what you see. Only over what you..." he freezes, his eyes becoming distant as if he's miles away. "It must be the repeated, prolonged exposure—"

"I said *stop*."

His gaze meets mine. I hate that he's still beautiful to me, that he's so familiar. So I desperately cling to the strangest thing about him: his eyes. Orbs of onyx, and deep within, swirls of red nebulae.

"I'm leaving," I announce, knowing how impotent I sound. But if he claims to want me safe, he'll let me go. He won't come after me.

I spin on my heels, toward the black door. Away from Dorian.

As far away as I can get.

It doesn't matter that *Pioneer's* comms array is gone. It doesn't matter that she has only drops of fuel left. I'll manage. I'll find a way, or I'll die alone on my ship. All I know is that I need to get out of this nightmare before Dorian's claws lodge in me for good.

Before I change my mind.

16

IMAGES ASSAULT me as I flee. The ghosts of my crew. Lily's skin peeling off. Dorian's eyes. The throbbing room that was his brain. I stumble through the corridors of this living ship, and it is no longer red and wet and bleeding, but still unbearably loud. The ship won't let me go, doesn't *want* me to go.

Thrum, thrum, thrum.

Dorian's words hang heavy over me. *The repeated, prolonged exposure.* How long have I been here? Days, months, years? It feels like days, but I know now that everything I've seen, even what I've felt, has been changed, warped, marred by this ship.

Not a ship.

A *lifeform*. Dorian himself.

If I've been eaten, I think, am I now in the act of being absorbed into this thing's bloodstream? Will I ever be able to, with a simple physical act, extract myself from the stomach, climb up the esophagus, and fall out of the gaping maw? Or am I here forever? Fleeing in circles, back to where I started until I forget myself altogether...

Footsteps echo behind me — Dorian? Or my mind playing tricks?

I glance over my shoulder and see him. He's the shadow that haunts me, the hell-black gaze that holds me. Even so, I hesitate.

No, Ami, I plead with myself. *Get out. Go.*

So I keep running. My lungs and muscles burn. The corridor is endless. I need to get to the docking bay. If I can just get to the docking bay...

Thrum, thrum, thrum.

A memory: I'm disembarking from *Pioneer*. Mahdi, Lily, and Vasilissa flank me as we descend the ramp into the docking bay. I gaze around me, taking it in, the vastness, the newness. My crew, my friends, vibrate with excitement. We're here, we made it. And someone's waiting to greet us: a man with pale skin and dark hair, with eyes as black as night.

The memory fades as quickly as it came. No, not a memory. A wish, a dream. A fantasy. My crew alive, all of us together.

His footsteps grow louder behind me.

"Leave me alone," I gasp, and push myself to keep running, though now it's more like a limping jog. My side aches, my lungs scream for air, and my heart is about to burst.

I come to a new corridor. I turn left, thoughtless, knowing I'm lost. Praying that I come to the docking bay. Praying *Pioneer* is still here, that I haven't imagined her, too.

Another memory: Vasilissa perching cross-legged on a bed. The room is small, orange-lit, and a pothos sits on the table in the corner. A viewscreen on the far wall shows a swathe of starlit space. I'm slouched across from her on the bed, head resting on my hand.

"This place," she says, her face twisting. "It's not normal."

I huff. "Of course it's not. It's an alien ship. What did you expect?"

Vasilissa leans toward me, her voice lowered, and there's fear in her eyes now, an intensity of emotion that chills my heart. "Don't you feel it?" she whispers. "You're different here. The way you look at him... and the way he looks at you. Something's happening to you, MiMi."

I sit back, defensive. "Don't call me that."

Vasilissa's eyebrows draw together, a line of concern forming between them. "Sorry," she says, not really meaning it. "But the others and I were talking, and we think it's best if you—"

The memory ends and I falter, my steps slowing.

No, *not* a memory. Vasilissa was never on the ship; it's another fantasy. But I don't want it, this isn't what I dream of. The ship is showing me things to keep me here, to frighten me into returning to its arms, so it can chew me up and swallow me whole.

My pace picks up again. His footsteps do too, and the endless hum never stops. It is my constant passenger, whispering horrors in my ear.

When the corridor opens up, and at last, the docking bay comes into view, I nearly fall to my knees and weep. My legs shake, my skull about to fracture from the ship's hum. But Dorian is catching up to me. I hear him coming, the clang of shoes against metal.

Get away, I have to get *away*.

And there she is, my escape: *Pioneer*. Docked and waiting.

I gather the last of my strength, preparing to make one last sprint to my ship, to freedom.

"Wait." Dorian's voice reaches out and holds me hostage.

He wants to keep me here, he wants all of me, my body, my mind, my soul. He wants to hurt me, to own me.

I hesitate.

"Ami, you can't leave."

I turn to face him, and he's gorgeous as a painting, Dorian Gray in the flesh, while I'm sweat-streaked and gasping, every muscle in my body screaming from exertion. "Let me go," I sob. "Let me *go*."

"I can't," he says, and as he nears, I see the swirls of red in his eyes, the smoky nebulae. He is the thrum, and the thrum is Dorian. "No matter how many times you try..."

I turn and sprint to *Pioneer*. My muscles threaten to tear, my heart to burst, my mind to crush under the weight of the thrum. *Stay, stay, stay,* it urges. But I resist. I reach my ship's hull and she is cool metal, real, and solid.

I press my palm to the control panel, and with a low whoosh of air, the ramp begins to descend. Escape is within my grasp.

And when I look to see if Dorian has followed me, a strange heaviness settles in my gut. He hasn't. He stands just inside the docking bay, watching me. Why is he letting me leave? Why isn't he trying to stop me?

It doesn't matter. I never want to see him again. I won't. I'd rather die slowly in the coffin of *Pioneer* than give in to him.

I make my way up the ramp, and my body nearly gives out. Even adrenaline can't keep me going forever. But I'm here. I'm almost free.

But once I'm safely inside *Pioneer*, the door sealed closed behind me, Dorian's voice caresses my brain. I hear him as clearly as if he's standing right next to me, soft lips brushing my cheek.

NO MATTER HOW MANY TIMES YOU TRY TO GO, YOU ALWAYS COME BACK.

17

LILY HOLDS me in her arms. I'm sobbing like a child, gasping, shaking with every breath, face blotchy and wet.

"It's okay," she says. "It's gonna be okay."

Her words have always been a comfort, her touch a soothing balm. But my pain is unending now. I can't fill my lungs; my heart is blown open and oozing, the shrapnel of its broken shell lodging sharp inside me. The sanitized lighting in *Pioneer* hurts my eyes. It smells wrong here. I *feel* wrong here.

"Let her be, Lills," says Mahdi. "You'll only upset yourself."

We're in the med bay. Mahdi comes to stand over us, where Lily and I are crowded together on one of the cots. He crouches so his eyes are level with mine. I'm sniffling now, no longer sobbing. I meet his gaze. There's something strangely hard in his expression, almost defensive.

"Listen, Ami." I can tell he's trying to be calm, but his tense jaw betrays him. "Whatever you're going through, it'll pass. Okay? It's just some kind of weird space madness.

You know this, right? He's not—" Mahdi's expression twists, and he looks away. "That thing on the ship," he continues at last, "it wasn't human."

"She knows that," Lily snaps.

I say nothing, but a black and seething rage boils up inside me. *That thing on the ship.* It doesn't matter what he is, whether he's human, alien, or something else entirely. They made me leave him. I had been desperate to stay, to know him, to be enveloped by him. He was everything to me. And they forced me to leave.

I remember now.

I refused to leave him. So my crew drugged me and carried me back to *Pioneer*. I woke up here. Dorian was gone. We left him far behind us, and I was alone. I'm still alone, even with Lily's arms around me.

Because I no longer hear the thrum.

"There, see?" Mahdi says, patting me on the shoulder, like I'm a broken-hearted teenager and he's my dad. "You'll be fine. Pretty fucked up though, if you think about it. What if we'd stayed longer? Who knows *what* that thing might have made us do, or feel, or forget."

More tears stream hotly down my face. I can't stop them. I'm alone. I left him. I'll never see him again.

"Go away," insists Lily, clicking her tongue at Mahdi. "You'll just make it worse."

Mahdi shrugs. "Just saying," he grumbles, getting to his feet. "You've seen her Psych Eval. I'd keep her under watch if I were you."

I'm descending the ramp from *Pioneer*. Mahdi, Lily, and Vasilissa flank me, and I feel the vibration of their anticipation all around me. We've just docked on an alien ship. This is our moment, the first contact. Our energy is palpable, our excitement like a drug. My heart flutters.

"How strange," says Vasilissa, slowly. "Does anyone feel like..."

"Deja vu?" Lily finishes for her.

Mahdi says nothing, but when I turn to look at him, his expression is miles away, his brow furrowed. I know what he's thinking: *Have I been here before?* Because I'm thinking the same.

Then a figure appears, emerging from the shadowy edges of the vast room. A pale man with black hair and even blacker eyes.

———

I'm on *Pioneer*. I'm shaking, blood-wet and sick. I try to make sense of what's coming back to me, these memories. They can't be real. It's another trick. My crew was never here. They died in stasis.

They died in stasis.

Bile rises in my throat as I make my way through *Pioneer*, leaving bloody footprints as I go, red streaks on the walls where I lose my balance and right myself.

"You're fine, Ami," I whisper, and know I'm lying.

No matter how many times you try to go, you always come back.

His words circle in my brain until they're a cacophony, razor-sharp agony, cutting at the tissue of my consciousness.

My hands shake as I settle into the cockpit, shutting off the viewscreen as soon as I do. I don't want to look out there. I don't want to see him. I flip all the right switches, check the readouts.

"*Pioneer*."

`Yes, Ms. Selwyn.`

"Do we have enough fuel, to..." I'm so shaken I can barely speak. I clench my fists and grit my teeth. "Do we have enough fuel to get out of this docking bay? Away from this ship?"

`Affirmative. But the fuel supply will—`

"Do it," I snap, cutting her off, even though the words are heavy on my tongue, resisting me. "Get me as far away from here as you can. I don't care if it depletes our remaining fuel."

`Affirmative.`

Empty, ghostlike, I stand. The sound of *Pioneer*'s engine coming to life, the warm rumbling below me, should fill me with relief. Instead, my head swims, and I'm caught up in thoughts of him, of the thrum. There's a gaping wound in my mind in the shape of Dorian's voice. Will distance make a difference, or will he always be with me?

I won't know when *Pioneer* begins her departure. Her inertia dampeners and the artificial grav make everything smooth and easy. But I can't sit around and wait for the engines to fire up; there's something I need to see. Just to be sure.

I climb down the ladder to the med bay. It's sterile and white, just as I remember. Cramped, claustrophobic, too clean. I enter the room, and glaring lights flicker on around me. Part of me had wondered if I would come here and find them gone, but they are just as I left them: Mahdi, Vasilissa, and Lily. Their faces are peaceful, as if sleeping. Zipped up tight, sealed in their stasis pods. They boarded *Pioneer*, and they never left. They never saw Dorian; they never entered his ship.

"*Pioneer*."

`Yes, Ms. Selwyn?`

I swallow hard, and it tastes like blood and bile. "Have we been here before?"

`Clarification required.`

"Have we docked on this ship before?"

`Affirmative.`

My gut turns to stone. "How many times?"

`Three times.`

"Three times we've been *here*?"

`Affirmative.`

I grip the edge of Mahdi's stasis pod. His gaunt face holds me in a death grip; I can't look away. "*Pioneer*, what happened to the comms array?"

`Unknown.`

"You *do* know!" I shout, looking wildly around, as if the ship's computer, a series of electrical impulses on a motherboard, will react to my fear and desperation. "Did someone tell you to lie?"

`Negative. I cannot lie.`

"*Pioneer*, did someone reprogram you?"

`Affirmative.`

I know the answer before I ask. "Who?"

`Unknown.`

I let out a guttural scream of frustration, and the med bay blurs around me, a thousand white lights flashing behind my eyelids, and I'm suddenly drowning in an onslaught of memories, back to back, crashing against me all at once:

A tiny, sharp knife. A scalpel in my hand. I know I should be afraid, that I don't know how to use one of these, where to slice and how, but I'm not. I've never been more sure of myself.

Dorian, holding me. We're naked, tangled together in my bed, back on his ship. "I don't want to go," I breathe, burying my face in his neck. He kisses my head. "You don't have to."

I'm suited up, outside *Pioneer*. Blackness surrounds me. I cling to the comms array with one hand. In the other, I hold an electrical saw.

I'm tethered outside the ship, still suited up. I'm at the fuel tank, meticulously opening it up. I'm watching as the fuel drifts out, brown-black globules fading into darkness, and I smile.

18

THE MEMORIES END.

Mahdi's lifeless countenance is beseeching in its silence. Not beseeching; *accusing*. I take a step back. Another. My heart hammers in my chest. I'm breathing too fast, too shallow; I know I'm hyperventilating. But there's nowhere to go.

I don't want to see them, the truth of what I know their bodies will show me. If I simply leave them here, all zipped up, the truth will remain: they died in stasis. I lost my mind on an alien ship. And soon, I'll die with them, of starvation or thirst or — most likely — hypothermia, when *Pioneer* eventually runs out of fuel and shuts down. It could be worse, I tell myself. It isn't such a bad way to go.

But, croons a traitorous part of myself, *you'll never see him again.*

"Fuck him," I say aloud, but it's weak. Unconvincing.

Turning, I lean over Lily's stasis pod. She is so beautiful there, so pristine. If I wanted to, I could open up the pod and press my fever-hot lips to her cold flesh. My chest aches. I miss her voice, her laugh, the way she saw how broken I was and loved me anyway.

I miss the way I loved her.

But maybe I'm only cut out for pain.

My thumb presses down on the stasis control panel, and with a soft hiss and a click, it unseals. I lift the glass slowly, almost reverent. Lily's eyelids are papery, her long lashes still so captivating. Holding my breath, I take hold of the zipper at her chin and pull it down to the collarbone, revealing her throat.

I lean close, so close I can smell antiseptic and the faint tang of death. And there it is: a precise mark, right along the jugular vein. A scalpel incision.

It's not surprise that renders me silent, or shock that keeps me from collapsing on the floor, that keeps me moving with slow determination. It's the certainty of suddenly knowing, of being helpless in the hands of a fate I've constructed.

I open Mahdi's stasis pod, lift the glass, and unzip the covering until his neck is revealed. His throat is open just like Lily's, a crisp line in the skin. And when I come to Vasilissa, I almost wish there was something I could do to change this. But there it is, stark and real upon her flesh: the incision I made.

I did it while they slept. No one woke, not one of them knew they were dying. I contained the blood as best I could, and when each of them was gone, I turned off the artificial grav and carried them one by one to the med bay. I cleaned their bodies, the floors, their bunks. I changed their clothes. I zipped them up in the pods, nice and tight, and I lay them to rest.

And then, finally, I was free to return. They wouldn't try to stop me again. They should have let me stay with him. If they'd only let me stay.

Mahdi was right. They should have locked me up.

Pioneer's engines power down.

I press my palm to the control, and with a hiss, her outer door swings open. The ramp descends, and I make my way down with careful steps. I'm standing in a docking bay, watching a man approach. He's strikingly beautiful, pale, with black hair framing a face that gleams with jet-black eyes.

He is painfully familiar, as achingly real and *right* as the breath in my lungs, the blood rushing through my veins.

He holds out a hand.

I go to him and take his fingers in mine, willingly, achingly. *Finally*.

He presses a soft kiss to my knuckles, his black eyes swirling with red haze. He smiles.

In the distance, a deep *thrum, thrum, thrum* sings through me, inside of me, filling my senses until I'm full of it, overflowing with it, overcome. But I welcome it, revel in it. And the sound responds in kind, caressing, soothing, soaking me in. I am part of it, made whole from it, completed by it. By *him*. And I am not afraid.

I am safe. I am home.

ACKNOWLEDGMENTS

I will try to keep this one short, to match the book.

Firstly, as always, thank you to Rachel Wharton, my editor, who would be horrified at my undoubtedly incorrect comma usage in this sentence. I can't imagine doing this author thing without you, Rach.

To Brooke Knight, for your unwavering friendship and always stellar advice.

To Logan Karlie, for being on this author journey with me and offering endless support when *Thrum* and I were at our lowest.

To the group chats (Lords of Writing and Meg's Pals): you are my everything.

Thank you to every reader who has cheered me on, encouraged me, expressed excitement, and injected my author career with joy. I do this for you.

Finally, thank you to my Adam, for being utterly perfect in every way. And for designing my covers.